Robert Bright Marston

Walton and Some Earlier Writers on Fish and Fishing

Robert Bright Marston

Walton and Some Earlier Writers on Fish and Fishing

ISBN/EAN: 9783337385835

Printed in Europe, USA, Canada, Australia, Japan

Cover: Foto ©Andreas Hilbeck / pixelio.de

More available books at **www.hansebooks.com**

WALTON

AND

SOME EARLIER WRITERS ON

FISH AND FISHING

BY

R. B. MARSTON

*Editor of " The Fishing Gazette" ; Honorary Treasurer of
the Fly-Fishers' Club*

" Companionable books, that tempt us out of doors and
keep us there."—JAMES RUSSELL LOWELL

ELLIOT STOCK, 62, PATERNOSTER ROW
1894

To

MY FATHER,

"THE AMATEUR ANGLER,"

I DEDICATE THIS LITTLE BOOK

IN REMEMBRANCE OF

DELIGHTFUL FISHING DAYS WITH HIM,

EXTENDING OVER MORE THAN

THIRTY YEARS.

INTRODUCTORY.

———

HAVE you read " The Compleat Angler" ? If you have, and are also acquainted with the Author's other writings, then these pages may perchance refresh your remembrance of them; but their object and the hope of the writer is to make Walton and a few earlier angling writers known to some to whom they are only names.

Looking back through a life, a never-failing delight of which has been the devouring of books, I confess that not many have had such an enduring charm for me as those of Walton. His " Compleat Angler" is the first book I can remember reading. I have the

vii

edition before me now, one of those pro-
ductions of the Chiswick Press, published
in 1863 by Bell & Daldy and Sampson
Low & Co.; and though I have seen
nearly all of the hundred or more reprints of the "Angler," and possess
most of the best, this little half-bound,
well-worn edition will always be among
those most prized.

I must have been born with a love
of angling. I certainly caught Prussian
carp in an old pond near to Craven
Arms in Shropshire long before I could
read. As a youngster of ten years I
remember one wet day wondering whether
any in that row of small books on the
top shelf of a book-case in my father's
library were interesting. Within reach
were rows of Scott in green cloth with
white labels; big volumes of Knight's
"History of England"; then a regiment
of Shakespeare in red; above them a
charming American edition of Dickens
in green cloth, published, I think, by
Ticknor, Fields, & Osgood. These and

many others were to be a discovery later
on. Who can forget the first coming
under the spell of the *Wizard of the
North,* or of Dickens, the *Wizard of
the South?* To me, then, these were only
repellent by reason of their big battalions.
But away above them was this row of
little books. I could just read the titles
of some from the floor. I remember
Southey's "*Nelson,*" White's "*Selborne,*"
George Herbert's "*Poems,*" Milton's
"*Paradise Lost.*" These did not appeal
much to a schoolboy's idea of books to
read. But suddenly I noticed in gold
letters the word "*Angler,*" and from the
top of a chair I saw the full title was
"*Walton and Cotton's Complete Angler.*"
By George! perhaps that's about fishing,
I thought; and stepping from the chair
on to the smooth, rounded, mahogany
cover of the writing-desk which formed
the lower half of the book-case, I clutched
the little volume, and then came down
with a crash on the floor. It was some
little time before I felt equal to opening

*my find; but when I did, and found I
had got three hundred pages about fish
and rivers and ponds, I forgot my
bumps, I forgot everything as I listened
to the voice of the dear old Master. If
I had only studied my school-books as I
did Walton! I remember some years
after, one hot summer day, when my old
schoolmaster, the Rev. Mr. H——,
was perspiring with the heat and his
endeavour to make some lines of Xenophon's "Anabasis" clear to a fat Irish
boy, that, thinking his attention would
be engaged for some time, I propped up
the lid of my desk as a screen, and was
soon deep in dearly beloved Walton.
The loud voice of the master and the
hesitating answers of the boy soon faded
away, and I was watching Piscator kill
that big chub with the white spot on his
tail, when bang went the master's cane
on his oak desk. I looked round my
sheltering desk-lid only to find, in perfect
silence, the whole eyes of the class on me,
and then, with Xenophon upraised in*

hand ready to hurl at my head, came the thundering " Marston ! what book have you got there ? "   Prepared at any moment to avoid Xenophon by a judicious " duck down," I said, " Please, sir, it's Walton's ' Complete Angler.' "   " Walton's ' Angler,' " repeated the master, and a pleasant change came over the flushed and angry but always jolly face.   " Come up here, sir, and let me look at it."   I went up with some misgivings, for the four-foot cane was not put down with Xenophon ; in fact, " old H——," as we irreverently called him, seemed to be trying its balance as he would a fly-rod. " Ah ! a very pretty edition" ; and after some little time, " And are you a fisherman ? "   I proudly said I was ; and then we had a regular talk about fishing, and I related how during the recent holidays I had lost a five-pound chub.   " What, sir ! How do you know he was five pounds, if you lost him ? "   " Well, sir, I think —I believe he would have weighed near six, if I had caught him."   " That will do, sir"; and with, as I thought, a half-suppressed twinkle in his eye, "Don't let me catch you again." After school, when we were talking about my escape, some of the fellows said, "Didn't you know he was a fisherman? Well, if you want a holiday any time, tell him you're going fishing, and if that don't fetch him nothing will." I had only recently been moved up into Mr. H——'s class, so I was not aware that he was as keen an angler as he was jolly and kind-hearted—though cane he could, and did. When morning lessons were half through, each master liberated his class for a quarter of an hour. At the end of the fifteen minutes a bell rang, and we of H——'s class knew if we did not clear out of the playground at once we should have to "run the gauntlet!" Mr. H——, in his college cap and gown, stood at the side of the open door. We had to rush past one at a time, and endeavour by fleetness or strategy to avoid the flying cane. Never was the wisdom of "festina lente" more impressed on one; for the greater your speed in endeavouring to escape the cane, the faster the master must make his cut to avoid missing the victim. It was better *to hasten slowly in close single file —better for all but the last man!*

One of my first essays in fly-fishing was for dace in the Thames from the meadows opposite Kew Gardens. These meadows are intersected by deep dykes. There was a school of girls walking along the towing-path on the opposite side of the river. As I was moving along the bank, I suppose I must have been looking at the girls, or I should not have suddenly gone bodily into a dyke six feet deep. Luckily, the tide was low, and the mud was soft; but I did not venture to reappear until the ripples of laughter from across the water had grown faint in the distance. But I caught some fine dace, I remember; for on my way home, when I got to Waterloo Bridge, which then had a toll-gate on it, I had not even a half-penny to pay the gate-

keeper. But St. Peter is the friend of fishermen, and the offer of some silvery dace in lieu of toll-money was accepted with alacrity.

I have mentioned these small matters because I think if one undertakes to give some account of a favourite author, it will not, at any rate, lessen any interest in what you write, if you can show that your acquaintance with the subject is a familiar one; and I think I may claim to know something practically about angling, from fly-fishing for salmon down to sniggling for eels. Every holiday I have had has been spent in some part of these beautiful Islands,—often after the big wary trout and grayling of Hampshire and other south-country streams, many times to the sweet south country which divides the Bristol from the English Channel, among the vales and dales of Derbyshire and Yorkshire, in the delightful Border country, among Scotch and Irish lake districts and Highland salmon

*rivers, through the Snowdon land, after
big pike in the Midlands; in fact, every-
where and anywhere that offered a chance
of good fishing. Nor have fish always
been the only object of my angling
expeditions: often enough it has been to
explore some delightful valley referred
to in some old writer, or to fish for rare
old books on angling in the old book-
shops. Beware of taking to collect books
on angling. You will find yourself become so attached to the fascinating hobby,
that you would, if necessary, pawn the
shirt off your back to obtain some coveted
edition. Not that one might not select a
thousand worse ways of investing time
and money than in forming an angling
library; for these little shabby volumes
of the sixteenth and seventeenth and of
earlier and later centuries are growing
in value at a marvellous pace.*

*There is a steady and increasing
demand in the United States of America
for old books on angling, and indeed
on sport generally; and it is pleasant to*

*know that the love of out-door sport of
all kinds is so strong among the sons
and daughters of the great Republican
branch of the Anglo-Saxon race. It is
this constant drain to America which
makes these books become scarcer every
year. When I first began collecting,
one could secure a good copy of the first
edition of Walton for £20 or £30.
Now it is worth five or six times as
much. The fact is, these books never
come back into the English market. An
Englishman makes a collection ; but
sooner or later he dies, and the chances
are that his collection is dispersed among
other English collectors by being sold at
auction ; and I am convinced it is not
so much the competition of English
collectors, as the gradual exhaustion of
the stock in this country by the Americans,
which makes old books on angling fetch
a higher price than any other class of
book.*

*Only the other day I purchased a fine
copy of Walton's second edition (even*

rarer than the first) : *its late owner would not part with it until he had my assurance that it was for my own collection, and not to go to America.* "*I do not see,*" *he said,* "*why all our rarest books should go to America.*"

It may be well to warn collectors that there exist some uncommonly clever spurious editions of Walton, made by aid of photography in Germany. When I say clever, they would not deceive any one who had any acquaintance with a genuine first edition ; but few of the many hundreds of collectors have any chance of seeing that, and I know from experience that there are unscrupulous second-hand booksellers. On one occasion, when passing an old book-shop, I looked in, as usual, to see if any fishing-books were for sale. After being shown some common modern editions, the bookseller remembered he had an old Walton upstairs—a first edition. He could not find it, but promised to send it on. The price was ridiculously low, if it proved

b

in good condition; and I congratulated myself on having secured a "find." But the book never came; and on calling for it, I was informed there was doubt about its genuineness. There was none until I gave my address.

The art of photography has rendered the manufacture of spurious "early editions" a game worth the candle, so that a word of warning in this respect will not be out of place. I was asked £25 for one worth about 5s. only the other day.

For this little work generally I will only claim that it deals at greater length with the principal works referred to than is the case in any other single volume. It would have been easy to give many more references in praise of Walton and his writings, but "enough is as good as a feast." That it is published in the three hundredth year since Walton's birth is an accident: it was begun before that "tercentenary" was thought of by me. Indeed, although I have printed on the front of " The Fishing Gazette" the date of Walton's birth and death every week for getting on for twenty years now, it was not until Dr. Henshall, who has charge of the angling exhibit at the Chicago World's Fair, wrote to me a month or two ago to say that they intended to celebrate Walton's birthday (as described in his letter to me, quoted on p. 104*), that my attention was drawn to the interest connected with* August 9th, 1893.

R. B. M.

Richmond, Surrey,
April 1894.

CONTENTS.

CHAPTER VIII.

CHAPTER IX.

CHAPTER X.

CHAPTER XI.

CHAPTER XII.

CHAPTER XIII.

WALTON'S "COMPLEAT ANGLER."

A SONNET BY T. WESTWOOD.

WHAT, not a word for thee, O little tome,
Brown-jerkined, friendly-faced—of all my books
The one that wears the quaintest, kindliest looks—
Seems most completely, cosily at home,
Amongst its fellows.   Ah ! if thou couldst tell
Thy story—how, in sixteen fifty-three,*
Good Master Marriot, standing at his door,
Saw Anglers hurrying—fifty—nay, threescore,
To buy thee, ere noon pealed from Dunstan's
    bell :—
And how he stared and . . . shook his sides with
    glee.
One story, this, which fact or fiction weaves.
Meanwhile, adorn my shelf, beloved of all—
Old book ! with lavender between thy leaves,
And twenty ballads round thee on the wall.

* 1653, *the date of the publication of* "*The Compleat
Angler*" *in St. Dunstan's Churchyard.*

WALTON AND SOME EARLIER WRITERS ON FISH AND FISHING.

CHAPTER I.

Piers of Fulham, 1420—Adventure of Sir William Wallace—St. Patrick and some Fish and Snake Stories.

BLAKEY, in his *Angling Literature*—a most interesting and useful little work—quotes from a curious tract, taken from the original manuscript in Trinity College Cambridge, entitled *Piers Fulham*, supposed to have been written about the year 1420, and containing probably the earliest known reference to angling in English, but a very short one. The writer says he would never store stews with " pykes " or " breame " or " tenche," because, " be it closed never so well aboute," thieves are sure to steal them.

1

" But in rennyng ryvers that bee commone,
  There will I fisshe and taake my fortune
  With nettys, and with angle hookys,
  And laye weris and sprenteris in narrow
      brookys,
  Ffor loochis, and lampreyes, and good layk,
  I will stele off no mans a strayke."

Angling has long been known as " the
contemplative man's recreation." I always
thought this expression originated with
Walton, as it is the second title of his
Compleat Angler; but it appears, from a
few lines of preface to the tract of Piers
of Fulham on fishing, this is not so :—

" Loo, worshipfull sirs, here after ffolle-
weth a gentlymanly tretyse full convenyent
for contemplatiff louers to rede and under-
stond, made by a noble Clerke Piers of
ffulhā, sum tyme ussher of Venus Schole,
which hath brieflye compyled many praty
conceytis in loue under covert terms of
ffysshyng and ffowlyng."

Adventure of Sir William Wallace while Fishing in Irvine Water.

Another early reference to angling, or at
any rate taking fish for sport, is found in
The Adventures of Sir William Wallace,
written about 1460 by a wandering Scotch
bard called Blind Harry. The incident

took place about a century and a half before Blind Harry's time, so that his account may be looked upon as made up from the traditions current among the Scotch people about their national hero. From an angler's point of view, it is pleasant to think of the great warrior Wallace turning to fishing for recreation, as did Washington and our hero Nelson.

Wallace, near the commencement of his career, is living in hiding with his uncle, Sir Ranald Wallace, of Riccarton, near Kilmarnock. To amuse himself, he goes to fish in the river Irvine, when this fishing adventure takes place.

> " So on a time he desired to play
> In Aperil the three-and-twenty day,
> Till Irvine Water fish to tak he went;
> Sic fantasy fell into his intent."

Wallace had good sport. " Happy he was, took fish abundantly "; but presently, some of the retinue of Lord Percy, who was then captain of Ayr, seeing Wallace's success, demanded his fish of him. Wallace meekly replied,—

> " It were reason, methink, ye should have part;
> Waith should be dealt, in all place, with free heart."

But they are not satisfied with part of the waith (spoil taken in sport), but take all, and derisively offer Wallace permission to catch more. The upshot of the affair is that five of his opponents attack Wallace, who kills three of them ; the other two escape, and complain to Lord Percy, who inquires how many were their adversaries.

"The Lord speirit, 'How mony might they be ?'
    'We saw but ane, that has discomfist us all.'
    Then leugh he loud, and said, 'Foul mot you fall !
    Sin' ane you all has put to confusion."

And scornfully declines to have Wallace pursued.

ST. PATRICK AND FISH AND SNAKE STORIES.

Ireland has not contributed very largely to the literature of angling, although from a song quoted by Blakey, written nearly a hundred years ago by an angler of Trinity College, Dublin, it would seem that St. Patrick was an angler. He sings :—

"No doubt, St. Patrick was an angler
        Of credit and renown, sir,
    And many shining trout he caught
        Ere he built Dublin town, sir.
    And story says (it tells no lies)
        He fish'd with bait and line, sir ;
    At every throw he had a bite
        Which tugg'd and shook the twine, sir.

    In troubl'd streams he lov'd to fish ;
        Then salmon could not see, sir ;

The trout and eels, and also pike,
  Were under his decree, sir.
And this perhaps may solve a point
  With other learned matters, sir,
Why Irishmen still love to fish
  Ever in 'troubl'd waters,' sir."

In a copy I picked up at an old book-
shop of Swift's translation of Jocelin's
*Life and Acts of Saint Patrick, the Arch-
bishop, Primate, and Apostle of Ireland,*
printed—and most beautifully printed—in
Dublin in 1809, is a copper-plate copy
of the three portraits drawn by Father
Thomas Messingham, and prefixed to his
Florilegium (Paris, 1624). The portraits
are of St. Columba, St. Brigida, and St.
Patricius. St. Patrick is in the centre,
standing on snakes and dragons. Among
the miracles attributed to St. Patrick is
that of the "river sentenced to perpetual
sterility." It appears that the Saint and
his companions having landed at the port
of Innbherde, in Leinster, where is a
river flowing into the sea, which river
then abounded with many fishes, the ser-
vants of the Saint asked the fishermen,
who were drawing their nets full of fish
to land, to bestow on them some of their
fishes. "But they, barbarous, brutal, and
inhuman, answered the entreaty, not only
with refusal, but with insult. Whereat

the Saint, being displeased, pronounced
on them this sentence, even his maledic-
tion, that the river should no longer produce fishes. . . . From that day, therefore,
is the river condemned to unfruitfulness."
On another occasion the Saint condemned
the river "which is called Seyle," near
the place called Tailltion, to perpetual
sterility, on account of somebody's sins,
and the chronicle adds that the river
"even to this day beareth no fishes."

In another chapter, which I quote from
only for the beauty of one or two expres-
sions in it, we are told how the Saint
persuaded to heaven the two daughters of
Leogaire, who were "like roses growing
on a rosebed : and the one was of a ruddy
complexion, and she was called Ethne ;
and the other was fair, and she was called
Fedella,"—who died, "and their friends
and their kindred gathered together and
bewailed them for three days, as was the
custom of the country ; and returned their
sacred remains unto the womb of the
Mother of all human kind."

Irish fishermen seem to have been very
stingy in their dealings with St. Patrick.
When he was journeying round Connactia
preaching, he came to the river Dubh,
and entreated the fishermen that out of
a great draught of fishes which they had

taken they would give him some, but they "wholly refused him even one fish"; so the Saint deprived the Dubh of its perpetual abundance of fishes, and enriched another river therewith, called the Drabhaois; "and this river, as being more fruitful, so is it clearer than all the other rivers in Ireland."

Another fish story connected with St. Patrick relates how one of his assistant preachers, Bishop St. Mel, having fallen under unjust suspicion, proved his innocence by "ploughing up the earth on a certain hill, and took by the ploughshare many and large fishes out of the dry land." St. Patrick accepted the miracle as a proof of his bishop's innocence, but "bade him that he should thenceforth plough on the land and fish in the water."

How St. Patrick rid Ireland of Snakes and other Poisonous Creatures.

"Even from the time of its original inhabitants did Hybernia labour under a threefold Plague: a swarm of poisonous creatures, whereof the number could not be counted; a great concourse of Daemons visibly appearing; and a multitude of Evil-doers and Magicians. And these

venomous and monstrous creatures, rising
out of the earth and out of the sea, so
prevailed over the whole Island, that they
not only wounded men and animals
with their deadly sting, but slayed them
with cruel bitings, and not seldom rent
and devoured their members. And the
Daemons, who by the power of Idolatry
dwelled in superstitious hearts, showed
themselves unto their worshippers in
visible forms; often likewise did they, as
if they were offended, injure them with
many hurts; unto whom, being appeased
with sacrifices, offerings, or evil works,
they seemed to extend the grace of health
or of safety, while they only ceased from
doing harm. And after was beheld such
a multitude of these, flying in the air or
walking on the earth, that the Island was
deemed incapable of containing so many;
and therefore was it accounted the habita-
tion of Daemons, and their peculiar possession. Likewise, the crowd of Magicians,
Evil-doers, and Soothsayers had therein
so greatly increased, as the history of not
any other Nation doth instance."

"And the most holy Patrick applied all
his diligence unto the extirpation of this
threefold Plague; and at length by his
salutary doctrine and fervent prayer he
relieved Hybernia of the increasing mis-

chief. Therefore he, the most excellent Pastor, bore on his shoulder the *Staff of Jesus*, and aided of the Angelic aid, he by his comminatory elevation gathered together from all parts of the Island all the poisonous creatures into one place :—then compelled he them all unto a very high promontory, which was then called Cruachan-Ailge, but now Cruachan-Phadring; and by the power of his word he drove the whole pestilent swarm from the precipice of the mountain, headlong into the Ocean."

CHAPTER II.

The Celebrated *Treatyse of Fysshynge wyth an Angle* Attributed to Dame Juliana Berners, 1496—Bibliographical Account of It—Its Practical Value from an Angler's Point of View—Considered as an Angling Idyl.

INASMUCH as nothing of the kind preceded it, and all later works are in some measure indebted to it, either for form or matter, *The Treatyse of Fysshynge wyth an Angle*, attributed to Dame Juliana Berners, must be accounted one of the most interesting, if not the most interesting, of books on angling in the English language.

It was in 1486, a few months after the last battle of the Wars of the Roses, when Henry Tudor, Earl of Richmond, was proclaimed King of England as Henry VII. on Bosworth field, that "The Schoolmaster of St. Albans" printed *The Book of St. Albans*, the first sporting work in the English language. It is divided into three parts : the first part treats of Hawking, the second of Hunting, and the third of Coat-Armour. Ten years later, in 1496, Wynkyn de Worde issued a second edition of *The Book of St. Albans,* adding a fourth part, *The Treatyse of Fysshynge.*

Sir John Hawkins, in his "Life of Mr. Isaac Walton," prefixed to his fourth edition of *The Compleat Angler* (1784), thus refers to *The Book of St. Albans* :—

"This tract, intitled *The Treatyse of Fysshynge wyth an Angle,* makes part of a book, like many others of that early time, without a title ; but which, by the colophon, appears to have been printed at *Westminster,* by *Wynkyn de Worde,* 1496, in a small folio, containing a treatise on *hawking,* another on *hunting,* in verse ; the latter taken, as it seems, from a tract on that subject, written by old Sir Tristram, an ancient forester, cited in the forest laws of *Manwood,* chap. iiii., in sundry places ; a book wherein is determined the *Lygnage of Cote Armures,* the above-mentioned treatise of fishing, and the method of *Blasynge of Armes.*

"The book printed by *Wynkyn de Worde* is, in truth, a republication of one known to the curious by the name of *The Book of St. Albans,* it appearing by the colophon to have been printed there in 1486, and as it seems with Caxton's letter (vide

Biographia Britannica, Art. "Caxton,"
Note L., wherein the author, Mr. Oldys,
has given a copious account of the book,
and a character of the lady who compiled
it). Wynkyn de Worde's impression has
the addition of the treatise of fishing, of
which only it concerns us to speak.

"The several tracts contained in the
above-mentioned two impressions of the
same book were compiled by Dame
Julyans, or Juliana Berners, Bernes, or
Barnes, prioress of the nunnery of Sopwell,
near St. Albans; a lady of noble family,
and celebrated for her learning and accomplishments, by *Leland*,* *Bale*, Pits, Bishop
Tanner, and others; and the reason for
her publishing it in the manner it appears
in, she gives us in the following words :—

" *And for by cause that this present
treatyse sholde not come to the hondys of
eche ydle persone whyche wolde desire it yf
it were enpryntyd allone by itself, and put
in a lytyll plaunflet, therefore I have com-
pylyd it in a greter volume of dyverse bokys
concernynge to gentyll and noble men, to the
entent that the forsayd ydle persones whyche
sholde have but lytyll mesure in the sayd
dysporte of fysshyng sholde not by this
meane vtterly dystroye it.*"

* This is said to be a mistake, as he does not
mention the name.

It is evident that Hawkins obtained this information about Dame Juliana Berners from Oldys.

Mr. William Blades, in his most interesting "Introduction" to Mr. Elliot Stock's very fine facsimile reprint (1881) of *The Boke of St. Albans*, devotes some pages to the work of demolishing the claims which for over a century have been made on behalf of Dame Juliana Berners by biographers and editors of the celebrated *Boke*. He says there is "not the shadow of evidence" that she wrote *The Treatyse of Fysshynge*, and "not a particle of evidence that she ever presided over the nunnery of Sopwell"; and yet Mr. Blades appears to think that she existed, for on another page he says, "that the greater portion of the book on Hunting was compiled by Mistress Barnes is probably correct." But whoever gave us the treatise of fishing makes no claim to have written it. He or she distinctly says, "I have compyled it." Mr. Van Siclen, who edited an American reprint, thinks it may have been written by Dame Juliana, because only a woman could have given such directions for making a rod, and that no man could have been guilty of "so delightful a *non sequitur* in many of the arguments"; which, as another editor* says, is "an ungallant hypothesis."

Sentimental reasons apart, it seems to me that Dame Juliana Berners has a better claim to be considered the compiler of the first English work on fishing than any one else ; for no claim is made for any other body ; and until such claim is made and substantiated, let us believe that the teacher of Walton was this "*Fœmina illustris! corporis et animi dotibus abundans ac formá elegantia spectabilis.*"

For a most careful and minute description of the various reprints of *The Book of St. Albans* and *The Treatyse of Fysshinge*, see Westwood and Satchell's invaluable *Bibliotheca Piscatoria*—a work without which it may most truly be said no angling library is complete. Alas that both compilers are dead, and no one has, so far, continued it !

---

* "*Treatyse of Fysshynge wyth an Angle.* Edited by Piscator. Privately printed. Edinburgh, 1885." A dainty little edition translated from the old black letter of the original into present-day typography, but containing such errors as "below" for "yellow," "dysporte" for "dystroye," etc. But the most desirable of all the reprints is the facsimile reproduction published by Mr. Elliot Stock, with a most pleasant "Introduction" by an angler and well-known angling writer—the Rev. M. G. Walkins, M.A.

THE "TREATYSE" FROM AN ANGLER'S POINT OF VIEW.

It is nearly four hundred years since this charming little *Treatyse* was first pub lished, and it has often been more or less gently ridiculed by writers who have judged it by the "rudeness" of the illus- trations or the "quaintness of its ortho- graphy," rather than by the value of its descriptions of rods, tackle, baits, and how and when to use them.

The author's reputation as an instructor in the art of angling would have been much higher than it has generally been rated if the illustrations had been omitted. They have been reproduced over and over again in works on angling, merely for the purpose of showing what a vast difference there is between our modern tackle and that apparently in use at the time of this writer; but it is possible that Wynkyn de Worde, thinking to increase the value of the work he was reprinting, added the illustrations—certainly there is nothing in the text to give one the idea that such coarse hooks, lines, leads, etc., were used.

The Rod.

The instructions given, if followed out at the present day, would produce a well-seasoned rod in three pieces,—the butt hollow, of hazel, willow, or aspen, with a ferrule to receive the second joint, which is to be of hazel, with a " fair shoot of blackthorn, crab-tree, meddler, or juniper " spliced to it for top joint.

The wood for the rod is to be cut between Michaelmas and Candelmas—*i.e.*, in the winter. The wood is to be " set " straight in a hot oven (as you may any day see the Redditch and other rod-makers do it in this year 1893), allowed to cool and dried for a month, then fastened to a large straight piece of wood, and the butt hollowed out, first by passing a red-hot iron through the pith, and after that enlarging the hole by many larger irons, and so tapering it. The butt is then to be allowed to cool, and after two days is unfastened and smoke-dried in the roof until thoroughly dried. The other joints are to be seasoned in the same way, and you thus get a rod which " will be light and full nymbyll to fish with." What is there in such a rod to laugh at ?—a light hollow butt, a springy second joint spliced to a fine tough top ; for the words " take a fair *shoot* of blackthorn," etc., show clearly no stiff weaver's beam of a rod is intended, such as that depicted in the printed work.

The Line.

For fastening the line to the rod an excellent plan is recommended, and one still in use among anglers who do not use a running line,—and your " crack " Lea roach angler disdains to use such an aid in killing his fish. Instead of fastening the line merely to the extreme point, you are to secure a piece of line to the splice between the top and the second joint, and then carry it down to the point and make a loop to fasten your main line to, the object being to reduce the risk of losing fish and tackle if the fine top should break, as the line would still be fastened to the stouter wood at the splice.

Recipes for colouring horsehair yellow, brown, green, tawny, russet, and dusky colours are given. Walton, more than a century and a half later, reproduces some of them almost word for word and without acknowledgment. What ! dear old Izaak among the plagiarists ! But more of this when we come down to his time.

Then we are told how to twist horse-hairs together to make a line, and the number of hairs to use for various kinds of fish, thus :—

2

For minnows	1 hair.
For small roach, bleak, gudgeon, and ruffe .	2 hairs.
For dace and large roach	3 hairs.
For the perch, flounder, and small bream, or "bremet," as it is here called	4 hairs.
For the chub, bream, tench, eel	6 hairs.
For the trout, grayling, barbel, and great chub	9 hairs.
For the great trout, with	12 hairs.
For the salmon, with .	16 hairs.
And for the pike . .	with a chalk line, armed with a wire at the end.

The Hook.

Dame Juliana gives detailed instructions in the manufacture of hooks, and the coarse illustrations in the *Treatyse* are again a libel on the text; for she recommends for small fish that the hooks should be made of the finest steel needles you can find; those for larger fish of larger needles, such as those used by embroiderers, tailors, and shoemakers. She mentions the spear-pointed shoemaker's needle, perhaps thus anticipating by four centuries the bayonet-pointed hooks and gaffs for

which we anglers of the present day have
to thank that genial angler and angling
writer Dr. John Brunton, M.A.

We are told how to soften these needles,
barb them, shape them, and re-temper
them, and then how to fasten the line to
them, so that the latter is bound on *inside*
the shank next the point, and not outside
—a bit of advice which has been repeated
by almost every angling writer after her.

Leads and Floats.

Here again the illustrations—rough
woodcuts as they are—do no manner of
justice to the text. The leads are to be
made round and smooth, so that they do
not catch on stones or weeds, and in size,
are to be regulated according to the nature
of the fishing, and are to be only " so
heavy that the least pluck of the fish "
pulls the float down.

The instructions for making floats have
never been improved upon ; indeed, only
the other day one of the best roach
anglers living * sent me some floats of his
own make which seem to me to be formed
exactly on the lines laid down by Dame
Juliana. She says :—

" Take a good cork which is clean

* Mr. E. J. Walker, of the Piscatorial Society.

without many holes, and bore it through
with a small hot iron, and fit into it a
quill strong and straight. The larger the
float, the greater must be the hole and the
quill. Shape the cork large in the middle
and small at both ends, and specially
sharp at the lower end. Then make the
cork smooth on a grinding stone. And
for a line of one hair the size of the cork
should not be larger than a pea, for a
line of two hairs of a bean, and for a line
of twelve hairs a walnut ; and so every
line after the proportion."

An egg-shaped cork with a porcupine
quill through it, made in various sizes, is
to this day the best float an angler can
use. An idea of the sizes of the leads
she recommends is easily and accurately
obtained by considering what the floats
she describes will carry : one float is to
be the size of a pea, another the size of
a bean, another the size of a walnut—not
the leads, but the floats !

Baits.

Of these almost all that are best are
here recommended ; and indeed I think
that anglers of the present day might with
great advantage take a lesson from this
Treatyse and from Walton, and give the
the fish a greater variety to select from ;

instead of worms, paste, gentles, and gentles, paste, worms, why not try this for barbel, for instance?—

"Take some good fresh cheese, lay it on a board, and cut it into small square pieces the size of your hook. Then take a candle and burn it while on your hook till it be yellow, then bind it on your hook with silk."

Toasted cheese is good both for mice and men; then why not for fishes? It has a strong appetising scent, and is a clean, wholesome, pleasant bait to use.

If my little work was intended as a practical treatise on angling, I should quote all the baits for all the various fish given by Dame Juliana, for I am sure in the course of centuries we have forgotten much that might with profit be remembered; but I must only glance at her book, and point out that she is the first to mention fly-fishing,* and to give a list of flies for the fishing months of the year. She even notes that, among other baits for the salmon, "you may also take him with a fly in like form and manner as you do a trout or grayling"—adding, "but it is seldom seen."

* I am not unmindful of that artificial *hippurus* which the Macedonians used, but every writer on fly-fishing has cast that fly.

Fly-fishing must have been practised much earlier than the period of this *Treatyse*; for how otherwise would such a complete description of artificial flies for the different months have appeared in it? Nothing but gradual evolution extending over perhaps centuries could account for this list of the—

"XII. flyes wyth whyche ye shall angle to ȳ trought and grayllyng and dubbe lyke as ye shall now here me tell.

JULIANA BERNERS' LIST OF ARTIFICIAL FLIES.

"*Marche.*

"The donne flye, the body of the donne woll and the wyngis of the pertryche. A nother doone flye: the body of blacke woll: the wynges of the blackyst drake: and the Jay under the wynge and under the tayle.

"*Apryll.*

"The stone flye, the bodye of blacke wull: and yelowe under the wynge, and under the tayle and the wynges of the drake. In the begynnynge of May a good flye, the body of roddyd wull and lappid abowte wyth blacke sylke: the wynges of the drake and of the redde capons hakyll.

"*May.*

"The yelow flye, the body of yelow wull: the wynges of the redde cocke hakyll and of the drake lyttyd yelow.* The blacke louper, the body of blacke wull and lappyd abowte wyth the herle of y pecok tayle: and the wynges of y redde capon w^t a blewe heed.

"*June.*

"The donne cutte: the body of blacke wull and a yelow lyste after eyther syde: the wynges of the bosarde bounde on with barkyd hempe. The maure flye, the body of dolke wull, the wynges of the blackest mayle of the wylde drake. The tandy flye at saynt Wyllyams daye, the body of tandy wull and the wynges contrary eyther ayenst other of the whitest mayle of ȳ wylde drake.

"*Juyll.*

"The waspe flye, the body of blacke wull and lappid abowte w^t yelow threde: the winges of the bosarde. The shell fly at saynt Thomas daye, the body of greene wull and lappyd abowte wyth the herle of the pecoks tayle: wynges of the bosarde.

---

* Stained yellow (for the "May Fly").

" August.

" The drake flye, the body of blacke
wull and lappid abowte wyth blacke sylke :
wynges of the mayle of the blacke drake
wyth a blacke heed."

I have often thought I should like to
have a set of Dame Juliana's twelve "flyes,"
dressed neatly on eyed hooks, to try on
the trout and grayling of the Test and
Itchin. Is not that " June fly " she calls the
" Tandy fly " also meant for the May fly ?
" The body of tandy wool and the wynges
contrary eyther against the other of the
whitest mayle of yᵉ wylde-drake." This
light drake hackle, dressed so that the
feathers lie " contrary eyther against the
other," is our nineteenth-century May fly ;
and I like that "whitest mayle," for I have
killed more and larger trout with a very
light-coloured Egyptian goose wing than
with any other feather, and prefer it at
times to the softer and darker Canadian
duck feather.

" Yᵉ Redde Capon's Hakyll."

It is just four centuries since Dame
Juliana recommended a red capon or red
cock's hackle, and it is pleasant to find

that " The History of the Red Hackle " is
the title * of the second chapter of a very
delightful modern treatise on fly-fishing,
entitled *Favourite Flies*, by Mrs. Mary
Orvis Marbury, an American lady ; and
a very interesting chapter it is, showing
" how one little fly has held its name and
form from century to century." Most of
the writers of any note who have recommended a red cock's hackle for use in
the imitation of some natural or unnatural
fly are quoted, from Ælian's famous description, in his *De Animalium natura*, of
the artificial fly made by the Macedonians
from "feathers which grow under a cock's
wattles," down to Dame Juliana, Walton, .
Cotton, and the writers of our own day,
including Pennell, Halford, Pritt, etc.
The coloured plate of seventeen "hackle
flies " which illustrates this chapter is very
good indeed. If our authoress had
written nothing but this " History of the

---

* " *Favourite Flies and their Histories.* By Mrs.
Mary Orvis Marbury. With many replies from
practical anglers to inquiries concerning how,
when, and where to use them. Illustrated by
thirty-two coloured plates of flies (nearly three
hundred flies), six engravings of natural insects,
and eight reproductions of photographs. Boston,
U.S.A.: Houghton, Mifflin, & Co.; London:
Sampson Low, Marston, & Co., Limited, St.
Dunstan's House, Fetter Lane."

Red Hackle," she would have proved her title to an honoured place among the great army of angling writers.

But I must reluctantly leave this practical portion of *The Treatyse of Fysshynge* with just one more reference to the illustrations which have, as previously mentioned, been so often ridiculed. If they are considered as they should be, in connection with the instructions given as to the making of the various things they represent, they will receive anything but ridicule from a practical angler. Take the illustrations of hooks in different sizes; they are rough diagrams certainly, but admirable in shape, being far better adapted for both hooking and holding than some of our modern hooks.

The " Treatyse " as an Angling Idyl.

It is impossible for an angler who loves fishing as much, or perhaps more, for its delightful and inseparable connection with all that is sweetest in country life and natural scenery, than for itself, to read Dame Juliana's eloquent prologue in praise of angling without experiencing a feeling of love and veneration for this fair saint of the angler's calendar. Who shall say how much her simple words in praise of " good

dysportes and honest gamys " have influ-
enced the generations of English men
and women which have passed away since
this sweet lady's time ? Twenty editions
of it have been published, and it has been
quoted and copied times out of number.

" HERE BEGYNNETH THE TREATYSE OF FYSSHYNGE WYTH AN ANGLE.

" Salomon in his parablys sayth that a
good spyryte makyth a flourynge aege,
that is a fayre aege and a longe. And
syth it is soo: I aske this questyon.
Whiche ben the meanes and the causes
that enduce a man into a mery spyryte ?
Truly to my best dyscrecōn it semeth
good dysportes and honest gamys in
whom a man joyeth without ony repent-
annce after. Thenne folowyth it ȳ gode
dysportes and honest games ben cause of
mannys fayr aege and longe life.* And
therfore now woll I chose of foure good
dysportes and honeste gamys, that is to

---

* James Russell Lowell, one of the greatest
of American authors and critics, in referring to
Walton's hope, when eighty-three years of age, that
he should next year pay another visit to Cotton
and the Dove, adds: "This was in his eighty-
third year, and implies in him that longevity, the
taste for out-of-door sports, and of the muscle
to endure their fatigues which are almost peculiar
to Englishmen."

wyte: of huntynge: hawkynge: fysshynge:
and foulynge. The beste to my symple
dyscrēcōn why then is fysshinge : callyd
Anglynge with a rodde : and a lyne and
an hoke. And therof to treate as my
symple wytte may suffyce : both for the
sayd reason of Salomon and also for the
reason that phisyk makyth in this wyse.

"*Si tibi deficiant medici medici tibi
fiant: hec tria mens leta labor et moderata
dieta.*

"Ye shall vnderstonde that this is for to
saye, Yf a man lacke leche or medicyne
he shall make thre thynges his leche and
medycyne : and he shall nede never no
moo. The fyrste of theym is a mery
thought. The second is labour not out-
raged. The thyrde is dyete mesurable."

After a pleasant discourse of the dis-
comforts and disappointments which often
attend the hunter who "blowyth tyll his
lyppes blyster, and whan he wenyth it
be an hare full oft it is an hegge hogge,"
and the "fawkener who often leseth his
hawkes," our authoress says :—

"Thus me semyth that huntynge and
hawkynge and also fowlynge ben so
laborous and grevous that none of theym
maye perfourme nor bi very meane that
enduce a man to a mery spyryte : whyche
is cause of his longe lyfe acordynge unto

ẙ sayd parable of Salomon. Dowteles
theñe folowyth it that it must nedes be
the dysporte of fysshynge wyth an angle.
For all other manere of fysshynge is also
laborous and grevous : often makynge
folkes ful wete and colde, whych many tymes
hath be seen cause of grete Infirmytees.
But the angler may have no colde nor no
dysease nor angre, but yf he be causer
hymself. For he maye not lese at the
moost but a lyne or an hoke ; of whiche
he maye have store plentee of his owne
makynge, as this symple treatyse shall
teche hym. Soo thenne his losse is not
grevous, and other greyffes maye he not
have, savynge but yf ony fisshe breke
away after that he is take on the hoke ;
or elles that he catche nought : whyche
ben not grevous. For yf he faylle of one
he maye not faylle of a nother, yf he
doóth as this treatyse teechyth ; but yf
there be nought in the water. And yette
atte the leest he hath his holsom walk
and mery at his ease, a swete ayre of the
swete savoure of the meede floures : that
makyth hym hungry. He hereth the
melodyous armony of fowles. He seeth
the yonge swannes : heerons : duckes :
cotes and many other foules wyth their
brodes, whyche me semyth better than
alle the noyse of honndys : the blastes of

hornys and the scrye of foulis that hunters:
fawkeners and fowlers can make.

" And yf the angler take fysshe : surely
thenne is there noo man merier than he
is in his spyryte.

" Also who soo woll vse the game of
anglynge : he must ryse erly, whiche thyng
is prouffytable to man in this wyse : That
is to wyte : moost to the heele of his soule.
For it shall cause hym to be holy, and to
the heele of his body. For it shall cause
hym to be hole. Also to the encrease of
his goodys. For it shall make hym ryche.
As the olde englysshe prouerbe sayth in
this wyse :—

" ' Who so woll ryse erly shall be holy,
helthy, and zely.'   .

" Thus have I provyd in myn entent that
the dysporte and game of anglynge is the
very meane and cause that enducith a
man in to a mery spyryte, whyche after
the sayde parable of Salomon and the
sayd doctryne of phisyk makyth a floury-
ing aege and a longe.

" And therefore to al you that ben
vertuous, gentyll, and free borne I wryte
and make this symple treatyse followynge :
by whyche ye may have the full crafte of
anglynge to dysport you at your luste : to
the entent that your aege maye the more
floure and the more lenger to endure."

The practical instructions forming the bulk of the little work are then given, and it closes with

Dame Juliana's Exordium.

" Here followyth the order made to all those whiche shall have the vnderstondynge of this forsayde treatyse and vse it for theyr pleasures.

" Ye that can angle and take fysshe to your plesures as this forsayd treatyse techyth and shewyth you :

" I charge and requyre you in the name of alle noble men that ye fysshe not in no poore mannys severall water : as his ponde : stewe : or other necessary thynges to kepe fysshe in wythout his lycence and good wyll.

* * * * *

" And also yf ye doo in lyke manere as this treatise shewyth you, ye shal have no nede to take of other mennys ; whiles ye shal have ynough of your owne takynge yf ye lyste to labour therefore. Whych shall be to you a very plesure to see the fayr bryght shynynge scalyd fysshes dysceyved by your crafty meanes and drawen vpon londe.

" Also that ye breke noo mannys heggys in goynge abowte your dysportes, ne opyn noo mannes gates but that ye shvtte theym agayn.

" Also ye shall not vse this forsayd crafty dysporte for no covetysenes to then-creasynge and sparynge of your money oonly, but pryncyppally for your solace and to cause the helthe of your body, and specially of your soule.

     *   *   *   *   *

" Also ye shall not be to ravenous in takyng of your sayd game as to moche at one tyme, which ye maye lyghtly doo yf ye doo in every poȳnt as this present treatyse shewyth you on every poynt.   Wyche sholde lyghtly be occasyon to dystroye your owne dysportes and other mennys also. . . .

" Also ye shall besye yourselfe to nouryssh the game in all that ye maye : and to dystroye all suche thynges as ben devourers of it.   And all those that done after this rule shall have the blessynge of God and saynt Peter, whyche he theym graunte that wyth his precyous blood vs boughte."

And so endeth this "lytyll plaunflet," so full of the true spirit of sport. Would that it could be said of all our modern "gamys and dysportes" that they were pursued under the golden rules laid down by its writer.

CHAPTER III.

"*Samias.* Worse and worse, but how wilt thou live?

"*Epiton.* By angling; O 'tis a stately occupation to stand foure houres in a colde morning, and to have his nose bitten with frost before his baite be mumbled with a fish."—From *Endimion*, by J. Lilly, 1591.

ANY works on sport of a general character have been published in English, and, when angling has been included, we generally find that the author or compiler of the work has been content to take one of the existing books on the subject of angling, and make up his section on fishing from that,

usually without acknowledgment, and often, as the *Bibliotheca Piscatoria* says, " marring the matter taken by the clumsiness of the transfer."

This is said to have been the case with the first work published after the famous *Treatyse*—viz., Leonard Mascall's *Booke of Fishing with Hooke and Line, and all other instruments thereunto belonging. Another of sundrie Engines and Trappes to take Polcats, Buzards, Rattes, Mice and all other kindes of vermine and beasts whatsoever, most profitable for all Warriners, and such as delight in this kinde of Sport and Pastime. Made by L[eonard] M[ascall]. [Woodcut of fisher and fowler.]   London. Printed by John Wolfe, and are to be solde by Edwarde White dwelling at the little North doore of Paules at the Signe of the Gunne.   1590.   B.L. pp. 93, and folding plate 4to.* According to the *Bibliotheca Piscatoria*, other editions appeared in 1596, 1600, and 1601. There is a copy of the first edition in the British Museum.

THE PIONEER OF FISH CULTURE IN ENGLAND.

Leonard Mascall deserves special praise for the extremely valuable instructions in practical fish culture which he gives, the first of the kind published in English; in fact, he must be looked upon as the pioneer of fish culture and fish preservation in this country.

Westwood and Satchell's *Bibliotheca Piscatoria* was published in 1883, and its reference to Leonard Mascall's book is almost confined to the statement that he took it from Dame Juliana, and spoiled what he took; but this inadequate and somewhat unfair notice is amply atoned for by the excellent reprint of the work which Mr. Thomas Satchell published next year (1884) with a preface and glossary. This reprint is now out of print, and it was only by a fortunate accident that I discovered its existence, when looking over the catalogue of a private collection of angling books belonging to my friend Mr. W. B. Adlington, who very kindly lent his copy to me.

Having for many years advocated the introduction into this country of some of the Continental methods of fish culture— more especially with reference to what the Germans call summer spawning fish, to distinguish them from the salmon and trout which spawn in the winter months—I was delighted to find that Mascall had done the same thing four centuries ago. There is pretty clear evidence that his book was very little known, in the fact that the very simple methods of fish culture which he describes and illustrates are, as far as I am aware, not referred to by subsequent angling writers. Even North, in his very valuable *Discourse of Fish and Fish-Ponds*, 1713, would have much improved his work had he included in it some of the methods described by Mascall.

As Mr. Satchell clearly shows, Mascall took his directions for fishing with "hooke and line" bodily from Dame Juliana Berners; about half his *Booke* is made up in this way, but the remainder is most of it, I think, written from his own practical experience, with the exception of a few passages which he acknowledges as "thus much taken of Stephanus in French."

Mr. Satchell says: "How much of the rest of the book is the author's own (*i.e.*, beyond that taken from Dame Juliana), and how much is drawn from other sources, I have not been able precisely to ascertain, but chapters fifty-nine to seventy are, I find, taken from *L'Agriculture et Maison rustique de M. Charles Estienne, Docteur en Médicine* (liv. iv., chap. 13-18, 22-26), and the particular edition used appears to have been that 'A Paris,

chez Jacques Du-Poys, 1570.' This is
inferred from the headings of the chapters
—not continued in later editions—which
Mascall has preserved, and one of which
has been curiously mistranslated. This
is chapter sixty-six, p. 36, headed, ' To
make it drie.' The words in Estienne's
are ' Pour les seiches '—to take ' crayfish.' "

Not the least interesting of the hints
given by Mascall is that for taking eels
with " a proching hooke "—a method in
use to this day, and one with which as a
school-boy I have taken many a fine eel
in the daytime and in clear water.

Here is Mascall's description :—

" There is another kind of hooke, calde
a proching hooke, which is made without
a barke [barbe] ; this kind or manner of
hookes are to put in a hole in the banke,
or betwixt two bordes at a bridge or water,
or betwixt two stones where they lie
open, for there commonly lieth the great
Yeles, and if there bée any yéeles, they
will take it anon : which proch, is wier
whipt on a pack thréedes end, and covered
with a great worme, and therewith prochin
to the saide holes. . . .

" As soon as ye féele she hath the
baite, plucke away your rodde, for it doth
nothing but guide your proch into y^e

holes, and then draw softly your pack-thréed line, and hold a while, and he will yéelde—if you do plucke hastely he will holde so stiffe, ye shall breake your line, or teare his mouth : there holde hard still and at length he will yéelde, and come forth. And where ye shall sée any hole in the bottome of a brooke or river, there is like to lie an yéele, put there in your proch, and he will soon byte if he be there. Thus much for the order of the proch hooke to take the Yéele."

Mascall gives practical instructions not only how to take fish, but also "how to save and preserve" them "against such devourers and raveners as hath and will destroy them, as the Herne, Dobchicke, the Coote, the Cormorant, the Sea-pie, the Kingfisher and such like, and also the Otter."

To Catch the " Herne."

To take the heron, he recommends baiting a hook with a minnow or other small fish, and then fastening it to a "greene" line or line the colour of the water she haunts, and pegging it down, so that she may have to wade half a foot deep unto it, or else the kite or crow will soon have it.

To Take the Otter, or "Water Wolfe."

Very interesting, and evidently from practical knowledge, are Mascall's directions for making otter-traps, or "weles," as he calls them. From the excellent illustrations he gives there would not be much difficulty in constructing one of them; indeed, I hope to get Mr. Bambridge, of Windsor, whose capital osier eel-traps I have found most useful on the Itchen, in Hampshire, to make one for me, for the keeper tells me otters have been very busy among the trout and grayling. At the present time, as far as I am aware, only steel traps are used for taking otters, and I have often heard keepers complain that it is difficult to get a trap that will hold an otter. Again, these steel traps, like large rat-traps, are dangerous things to use, as ducks, geese, and other domestic birds and animals may be killed by them, or bathers seriously injured.

But if Mascall's otter "wele" is effective, it would be dangerous only to otters. I wonder if any descendants of those who made them in Mascall's time are living? He says: "'These Otter Weles are made at Twyford, by sides Reading. There be two of the Gootheriches which lives much

by making of such, and other Weles.
Also the Otter Wele is made at Dorney,
by Windsor, by one called Twiner." He
adds that "it should be made of good
round Ozyars of the Hasell rodde or gore
rodde, for those are the best."

In a few words Mascall's "wele" may
be described thus :—It is a double basket
trap made of strong hazel stick. At the
entrance to the inner compartment, containing the bait is a spring. The otter
creeps into the outer compartment and
on endeavouring to get at the fish releases
the spring and causes a "gredyern" [grid-
iron] door to fall, and so entraps him.
"As soon as he hears it fall, he will turne
back without touching any fish, gnawing
at the gredyern where he came in, and so
is drowned."

He warns the reader against using an
old "wele," as, if it is rotten and the otter
escapes, "ye shall hardly take him of a
long time after, for he is very subtill to
be caught againe in such a wele."

FISH CULTURE IN MASCALL'S TIME.

In view of the great strides made in
fish culture during the past thirty years,
it is interesting to find that some of the
methods so much advocated of late were

known centuries ago. I should like to see the following instructions printed and exhibited on the walls of all angling clubs.

To Preserve Spawn in Spawning Time.

" A chiefe way to save spawne of fish, in March, Aprill, and May, is thus :—Ye shall make fagots of wheate, or rie strawe, all whole strawe not bruised, or of reede. Bind these faggots together with three bondes, and all about thereon sticke of young branches of willowe. Then cast them in the water among weedes, or by the bankes, and put in each faggot two good long stakes, driven fast to the ground, and let your fagots lie covered in the water halfe a yeard or more. So the fish will come and shed their spawne thereon, and then it will quicken therein, so that no other fish can come to destroy or eate it, and as they waxe quicke they will come forth and save themselues.

" Thus much for the preserving of spawne in the spring and spawning time : this is a good practise to preserve the spawne of all scaled fish.

" These faggots ye may make and lay in all rivers, poundes, or standing waters. Your fagots had neede to be a yeard and a halfe long, and bound with three bandes not hard, two bandes a foote from the endes, and another band in the middest, and lay them as I have afore declared.

"Also some doe use to hedge in corners in rivers and pondes with willow, and thereon fish doe cast their spawne and so breedes."

An Ingenious "Manner of Way to Take Sea-Pies, Crows, and other Pyes."

Mascall gives an illustrated description of this. He says if you take two small "oziars" and bend them together crosswise near the end, and tie a bait to the twigs with a short thread, then lime the twigs and place them on some water weed or rush, or suchlike in the midst of the river, the birds will "flie away with it in their bylles, and soon they shall be lymed therewith . . . for the twigs will turne and touch her wings, and then the pye will fall." He adds that "you may take sea-pies, crowes, and other Pyes therewith, but that you will hardly catch the Kyte, because he takes the bayte in his feete, and the other takes it in their billes."

"Thus much for the taking of the Sea-pie."

Mascall's Opinion of the Flavour of " Frogges."

" In many places frogges, being well drest, they eate like fish, and is calde a kinde of fish, and doe taste as well as a young poullet, for I tasted my part of many."

He Advocates the Cultivation of a Fish now Very Rare in England —the " Poult " (Eel-Pout or Burbot *).

" There is a kind of fish in Holand, in the fennes beside Peterborrow, which they call a poult; they be like in making and greatness to the whiting, but of the cullour of the Loch [loach]; they come forth of the fenne brookes, into the rivers nigh there about, as in Wandsworth river †† there are many of them.   They stirre not all the sommer, but in winter when it is most coldest weather.   They are taken at Milles in Welles [eel-baskets], and

* The statement in the *Bibliotheca Piscatoria* that Franck (1694) is the first English writer on angling who describes that mystical fish the "burbolt" is incorrect, as my quotation from Mascall (1596) proves.

† The Wandle—not many years ago the purest chalk stream in England, now tainted by the water from Croydon's sewage farm, and polluted by village drainage.

at waters [weirs] likewise. They are a pleasant meats, and some do thinke they would be as well in other rivers and running waters, as Huntingdon, Ware, and such like, if those waters were replenished with them, as they may be with small charge.

"They have such a plentie in the fenne brookes, they feede their hogges with them. If other rivers were stored with them, it would be good for the common wealth, as the Carpe which came of late yeares into England. Thus much for the fenne pult."

This fish is now only seen occasionally in the Trent and a few other rivers.

There is not much order in Mascall's book ; in fact, it is a collection of notes thrown together in rather a haphazard manner, and, as previously mentioned, it it is not quite clear how much " is taken of *Stephanus* in French." But there is an English flavour about the names of places mentioned in his account of how

" TO BREEDE MILLERS-THUMBES AND LOCHES IN SHALLOW BROOKES OR RIVERS.

" The fish called Loches, and the other called Millers-thumbes or Culles,* they

* In Ireland the loach is called " colley."

always feede in the bottome of brookes, and rivers. They are fish holesome to be eaten of feeble persons having an ague, or other sicknesse." He then recommends that, in order to preserve these useful little fish from "water rats and all other fowles" rows of small heaps of stones should be placed in shallow gravelly streames. "Like as there is a shallow river running from Barcamstede to Chestum, and so to Chane: also by Croydon, and other places, wherein they might breede of the said fish great store, if they were so given. The like river runnes in Hampeshire bysides Altum, increasing by diverse springes, and runnes shallow in many places, and by a certaine parish there called   ; the Parson thereof hath tolde me, he hath had so many of the saide Culles and Loches, to his tithe weekly, that they have found him suffi- cient to eate Fridays and Saturdays, whereof he was called the

" Parson of Culles."

In the reprint from which I am quoting the name of the parish of the Parson of Culles is left blank: I know not if it is so in the original.

Mascall is probably following his French teacher when he tells us quaintly of the times and seasons when fish are "hole-some": for instance, that "Cockles and such are not kindly but in the monethes of March, Aprill, and May."

After relating how strictly the laws are enforced in France against the taking of under-sized fish, fish out of season, or destroying fish by unlawful means, he adds :—

"I WOULD TO GOD IT WERE SO HERE WITH US IN ENGLAND, and to have more preservers and lesse spoylers of fish out of season and in season : then we should have more plentie than we have through this Realme."

It is pleasant to know that, if Mascall could revisit "this Realme" and then journey through France, he would find that his comparison of the state of affairs as regards the inland fisheries would have to be reversed ; indeed, our rivers never were in such a sad state as are those of France now—netted, poached, poisoned, dynamited, fished to death, her grand salmon rivers and lovely trout streams now, alas ! too often utterly ruined. The chief de-stroyers of our inland fisheries are the manufacturer, the town councillor, and last, but by no means least, the sanitary authority.

CRAYFISH CULTURE.

Another interesting bit of fish culture is given under the heading " The breeding of Crevis." Our author says :—

" 'The fresh water Crevis, commonly lives and lyes in bankes and holes in rivers and brookes, and they are a holesome fish for all sick and weake persons. They will cast their spawne in the Spring about the moneth of May, and will shed it on stones, and weedes in the bottome, whereof most is eaten up with yeeles and water rats, as some suppose.

" Therefore it were not vnmeete to make fagots of hole straw to save the spawne as aforesaide. Also they will soone be driven with floods downe the streame, in few yeares they will greatly increase, if they be not taken with mens handes, and kild with Rats, for they will lie in holes and under stones, and weedes, and so are soone taken : for they cannot flie fast away. If they be taken in May it will be a great spoyle in their increase, for commonly they then doe shed their spawne. The Water-rat is also a great devourer of them lying in holes : and where many rats are, they cannot lightly prosper or increase there.

"Thus much for the fresh water ' Crevis.' Ye may store any brooke or river with them, but especially he loves the sandie and gravely running waters."

Mascall gives an excellent illustration of the crayfish—not quite equal to that in Professor Huxley's delightful monograph on the subject, of course, but excellent, considering the centuries between them. The gastronomical value of the crayfish is no slight one, as all will admit who have tasted it on the Continent in *Potage Bisque*, or as a garnish with fish, or simply boiled and eaten with salad and *mayonnaise* sauce. According to Professor Huxley, there are on the Continent two kinds of crayfish, whereas we have only one, and ours the least valuable of the two. I remember that in Germany we used to value the Edel-Krebs much before the Stein-Krebs, and in France the "Écrevisse à pieds blancs" is esteemed much less than the larger "Écrevisse à pieds rouges."

Some years ago I read an account in a German fishing paper of a great war which was said to be going on in Russian rivers between the noble crayfish and the stone or common crayfish, in which the former were being gradually exterminated. It is certain that the crayfish is subject to a very mysterious disease, called "crayfish pest," in Germany, by which it is extir-minated in whole districts. Like grouse disease, potato disease, and *saprolegnia ferax*, which has destroyed so many thousands of salmon yearly, and many other diseases called blights, we know little about it, and less how to cure it. In our English rivers crayfish are by no means common, and in those comparatively few in which they were formerly abundant they are now scarce. They are found still in large numbers in the New River, which in part supplies London with water, and were very abundant, and may be so still, in the Stoke Newington reservoirs of the New River Company. I remember one rather curious incident in which these strange little fellows played the chief part. It was one hot afternoon in the sixties. I was fishing from the sloping stone embankment of one of these reservoirs. The fish would not bite, and I was reading on the bank, when I heard a peculiar scratching noise. It went on for some time; and, on getting up to see the cause of it, I saw that hundreds of crayfish were crawling up out of the water on to the big stones. The noise was caused by their claws as they clambered upon the stones. I say hundreds, but there must have been thousands; for, on walking along the bank, I never saw such a sight before or since, and can only suppose that the water, on that particular day, had got too warm for them, and that they came out for a change. As I walked along the bank they clumsily scrambled back.

Mascall and the "Kinges Fisher."

A Curious Statement.

After describing how to catch a king-fisher with bird-lime, Mascall has this note: "Also they say this bird, being dead, if he be hanged up by the bill with a thread in your house where no winde bloweth, his brest will alway hang against the winde, whereby ye maye knowe perfectly in what quarter the winde is at all times both night and day."

The "Dobchicke."

Our English trout-river keepers are all unmerciful to the dabchick, or "Dobchicke," as Mascall calls it, and not without reason, if he is right. He says: "The Dobchicke will be always commonly on rivers and pooles, and they are nigh as great as the Teales, and are of cullour blacke, and they will commonly dive under the water to take young fish, as I have seene in rivers and brookes." And he then illustrates and describes a peculiar method of taking them, viz.: "The fishermen doe use to lay on the water long lines of small threede knit full of little corkes, a handfull a sunder on the line, and cut foure square like bigge dice, and so limed, and will spread the saide line afore them on the water, and then with their boats drive them to the say'd line, and so many are taken."

How often the trout-fisher, coming suddenly round the bend of the stream, has seen what he took to be the ring of a rise, and prepared to float his fly over the spot, when a little black head a few yards lower down bobs up, and he says to himself, "Only a blessed dabchick!"

Mascall gives what are doubtless excellent recipes for making bird-lime, and finishes his most interesting notes with one entitled

"A Pretie Way to Take a Pye.

"Ye shall lime a small threede, a foote long or more, and then tie one end about a piece of flesh so big as shee may flie away withall : and at the other end of the thread, tie a shoe buckle and lay the flesh on a post, and let the threede hang downe, and when she flies away with it the threede with the buckle will wrappe round her, and then she will fall, so ye may take them."

At the end of this excellent reprint of Mascall's most interesting book is a useful glossary. This reprint must be getting scarce, for I have not seen one mentioned in any second-hand book catalogue, and an advertisement for one in *The Publishers' Circular* brought no replies.

CHAPTER IV.

Michael Angelo an Angler—*La Canna de Piscare*
—Blakey and the *Bibliotheca Piscatoria*—
Mynheer Vandunk.

IN 1596 * a black-letter reproduction of *The Book of St. Albans*,
with considerable variations, was
published, entitled "*Hawking,
Hunting, Fowling, and Fishing*, with the
true measures of blowing, etc., by William
Gryndall, now newly collected by W. G.
Faulkner."

In 1600 appeared another black-letter
quarto, entitled "*Certaine Experiments
Concerning Fish and Fruite*: practised by
John Taverner, Gentleman, and by him
published for the benefit of others. London, printed for William Ponsonby,
1600."

Before coming to "*The Secrets of Ang-*

* My late friend the Rev. J. J. Manley, M.A.,
gives the date of publication as 1593 in his pleasant book *Notes on Fish and Fishing* (S. Low &
Co., 1877).

ling, by J. D.," which deserves far more notice than can be given to it in this little volume, I should like to direct the reader's attention to a few extracts from Blakey's *Angling Literature*, an extremely interesting book, now out of print, but not difficult to obtain through the second-hand booksellers. We know that some of our greatest living painters, including Sir John Millais, Mr. John Pettie, R.A.,* and Mr. Orchardson, R.A., are enthusiastic anglers, and I was delighted to find that

MICHAEL ANGELO WAS AN ANGLER :

that is to say, if the following extract from Blakey's book is correct. The Italian author was evidently a true Waltonian. I mean that, like Dr. Prime, he found far more in fishing than mere fishing :—

"In 1712 we find another Italian publication, of about two hundred and fifty pages, entitled *La Canna de Pescare*, in which there are some interesting descriptions of angling excursions on some of the higher sections of the river Arno and its smaller tributaries. 'I have travelled much,' says the author, 'with the rod, in certain seasons of the year, by the banks of the chief fishing localities of Italy, and

* Died since these lines were written.

I feel at all times as if I had made my
escape from the ordinary ills and plagues
of life. I have commonly had one or
two companions, and we have enjoyed
ourselves in as lively and rational a manner as possible; giving to Nature all her
due, and dwelling on the various pic-
turesque scenes we every day meet with,
in that true spirit of admiration so im-
provable to the heart and understanding.
I feel confident that most of our great
artists must have been fishers in early life.
Our art is well fitted to arouse the dormant
powers of sentiment, and the general ideas
of the sublime and beautiful in external
nature. It is said that Michael Angelo,
when a youth, often amused himself with
the fishing-rod, and would take long
journeys to visit spots famous for their
rural scenery and beauties. The same I
have heard remarked of less distinguished
artists, both sculptors and painters of our
own and other countries' (*La Canna*,
p. 60)." *

* In the *Bibliotheca Piscatoria* (1883) the only
reference to this work is as follows: " *Canna. La
Canna de Pescare,* 1612. (Known to us by title
only)."   Robert Blakey, whose preface to his
*Historical Sketches of the Angling Literature of
all Nations* is dated 1855, evidently knew the
book, or we should not have had this delightful
extract from it.

Blakey certainly made some very curious blunders in dates, etc., but I do not think many readers of his work will agree with Messrs. Westwood and Satchell's wholesale condemnation of it in the *Bibliotheca Piscatoria* as a "slip-shod and negligent work, devoid of all real utility." In his preface he says: "Whatever imperfections, either of commission or omission, which the volume may display, will, I trust, receive some degree of critical indulgence from the fact that this is the first attempt, as far as my knowledge extends, of anything of the kind in any language whatever." He adds: "I conceive it will prove of interest to all true Piscatorians." It is doubtless well to be precise about dates. I make it a rule to add the date to any undated communication I receive if it is of the slightest importance; but, after all, a date is only a date, and, if for nothing more than his extracts and translations of foreign works referring to fishing, Blakey's book must always be of interest and utility. In all the great list of the *Bibliotheca Piscatoria* none is mentioned which covers or attempts to cover this ground as he does. His other works, *Hints on Angling, The Angler's Complete Guide to the Rivers and Lakes of England, The Angler's Guide to the Rivers and Lochs of Scotland, The*

Angler's Song Book, etc., must always secure for him a place in the affections of those he calls "Piscatorians." At p. 109 of his *Angling Literature* he says: "The earliest caricatures of the angler we have seen bear the date 1603. One represents a Dutch amateur, evidently of some public notoriety, sitting like a lubberly clodpole, with the most bewildering expression of face, pulling a prodigious large salmon at the foot of a weir; in another print figures a fisher weeping for the loss of a part of his rod and tackle. Underneath the print are some verses, which may be paraphrased thus :—

"'Mynherr Vandunk, though he never got drunk,
  Sipp'd brandy and angled gaily;
And he quenched his thirst with two quarts
    of the first,
Hooking lots of fine salmon daily:
Singing, "Oh that a fisherman's draught could
    be
As deep as the rolling Zuyder Zee!"

" 'Water well mixed with spirit good store,
  No fisherman thinks of scorning:
But of water alone he drinks no more
Than to help him to bring his fish on shore
Upon the market-stall in the morning.
For a fishing Dutchman's draught should be
As deep as the rolling Zuyder Zee.'"

If this is one of Blakey's "quotations incorrectly given, and of so-called original passages the vagueness and uncertainty of which rob them of all weight and value," according to Messrs. Westwood and Satchell, all I can say is, "*Si non e vero e ben trovato!*"

CHAPTER V.

John Dennys' delightful *Secrets of Angling*, 1613
—Some Account of the Book and its Author
—A Parenthetical Reference to Multiplying
Reels and Sir Humphry Davy's *Salmonia*—
The *Secrets* compared with Dame Berners'
Treatyse — Quotations from the *Secrets*—
Angling in the Age of Wood, of Gold, of
Silver and Brass—Angling in the Iron Age.

EFERRING the reader for further
notices of Continental angling
literature of this period to Blakey's
book, I come back to England
and the year 1613, when " *The Secrets of
Angling*, by J. D.," first saw the light. For
nearly two centuries it was not clearly
known who was the author of this, in my
humble opinion, most charming poem in
all our English angling literature, and we
are greatly indebted to the authors of the
Bibliotheca Piscatoria for their very full
account of it and its various editions, and
of such particulars of its author as are

known, which I, with full acknowledgment to them, quote as follows :—

"This poem is also noticed, with large citations, in an article in the *Censura Literaria*, 1809, vol. x., p. 266, which was appropriated by Daniel * and inserted in the supplement to his *Rural Sports*, 1813. Its authorship was set at rest in 1811, by the evidence of the books of the Stationers' Company, in which the work is entered as being by JOHN

---

* On referring to my copy of the Rev. W. B. Daniel's *Rural Sports*, I find I am able to supply an omission in the *Bibliotheca Piscatoria*, which makes no mention of the edition I have—Royal 8vo, printed for Longman, Hurst, Rees, & Orme, Paternoster Row, 1807; also to correct an American angling writer, Mr. A. Nelson Cheney, who, in one of his pleasant angling Notes in *Forest and Stream; or, Shooting and Fishing*, January 1893, claims that the multiplier reel was invented in America about the year 1820. In this 1807 edition of Daniel's *Rural Sports*, not the first edition of the work, there is a fine engraving of a brass multiplying reel. I have no doubt multiplying reels were in use much earlier than this. In 1770 Onesimus Ustonson advertised that he sold "the best sort of multi-plying brass winches, both stop and plain"; he also advertised "superfine silkworm gut, no better ever seen in England, as fine as hair, as strong as six, the only thing for trout, carp, and salmon." The first mention I have found of the use of a reel at all is in *Barker's Delight*, 1651.

DENNYS, ESQUIRE. Sir Henry Ellis gives the extract (from the books of the Stationers' Company) in his edition of the poem published by B. Triphook, London, 1811."

The entry in the registers of the Stationers' Company is quoted in Mr. Thomas Westwood's very interesting "Introduction" to his edition of the *Secrets*, published by W. Satchell & Co., as follows :—

" 1612, Feb. 28th.* Mr. Roger Jackson entered for his copie under th'andes of Mr. Mason and Mr. Warden Hooper, a booke called *The Secrets of Angling*, teaching the choycest tooles, baites and seasons for the taking of any fish in pond or river, praktised and opened in three bookes, by John Dennys, Esquire. vjd."

Roger Jackson was also one of the publishers of Gervase Markham's *Countrey Contentments*, etc. Among other of his works, I have one dated the same year as *The Secrets of Angling*, viz. 1613, with this imprint :—

"Printed at *London* by I. B. for R. Jackson, and are to be sold at his Shop neere Fleete-Streete Conduit. 1613."

* According to others, March 23rd.

"Walton" (continues Mr. Westwood) "had previously ascribed the *Secrets* to John Davors, and others (Howlett among them) to Donne and Davies. The volume contains commendatory verses signed 'Io Daues,' and is dedicated by the stationer R. J. to Mr. John Harborne, of Tackley, in the county of Oxford.

"Beloe says of the book that 'perhaps there does not exist in the circle of English literature a rarer volume.' Sir John Hawkins confessed 'he could never get a sight of it.'

"There is every reason to suppose that Mr. John Dennys, who is shown by the pedigree of the Dennys family to have died at Pucklechurch, Gloucestershire, in 1609, is the real author of the *Secrets*, not the grandson of Sir Walter Dennys, put forward for that honour by Sir Harris Nicolas. No date is associated with Sir Walter Dennys, but, on referring to a more detailed pedigree from the same source, it appears that his eldest son, 'Sir William Dennys,' founded a guild in the year 1520. We may therefore reasonably assign his birth to the latter part of the fifteenth century, or to the very beginning of the sixteenth. These premises are borne out by the fact that John, his second brother (author of the *Secrets*, according to Sir

Harris Nicolas), left a son, Hugh Dennys,
who died in 1559, and at no immature
age, since he was married, and had
four offspring. If, therefore, Sir Harris
Nicolas's assumption be correct, we must
ascribe the poem to the early part, at
the latest to the middle, of the sixteenth
century, whereas its style and general character belong assuredly to a later period.

" Collateral evidence is to be found in
the fact that R. J. (Roger Jackson), in his
dedication, does not throw the poem far
back, in a posthumous sense, but merely
says : ' This poem being sent unto me to be
printed after the death of the author, who
intended to have done it, in his life, but
was prevented by death,' etc."

The *Bibliotheca Piscatoria* then quotes
a long and appreciative notice of the
poem by T. Westwood, published in
The Angler's Note-Book, 1880, pp. 181-85,
from which I shall take but a short
extract :—

" It is not needful that I should enter
into a critical appreciation of this little
poem, the finest passages of which are
well known and highly esteemed. Thus
much, however, may be said, that, so
replete is it, in its higher moods, with
subtlety of rhythm, sweetness of expression, and elevation of thought and feeling,

that, *even from the angling point of view,
we cannot but consider it a notable piece of
condescension, and marvel at the devotion
of so much real poetic genius to a theme
so humble.* With the exception of *The
Compleat Angler*, no higher compliment
than this poem has been paid to the
sport."

The italics in the quotation are mine ;
and surely all anglers will agree with me
that from any point of view our sport and
art can be considered "humble " is absurd.
The truth is, that the compilers of the
Bibliotheca Piscatoria were literary rather
than practical anglers : they fished very
successfully in the tributaries as well as
in the main stream of bibliographical
research. We must ever be deeply indebted
to them for carefully collected particulars
about the dates, sizes, editions, etc., of
books on angling, but their criticisms of
angling works and angling writers were
not always just. For instance, what angler
will agree with the remark that Sir Humphry Davy's *Salmonia* "lacks freshness
of heart "? This work was written as a
recreation by the author "during some
weeks of severe and dangerous illness,
when he was wholly incapable of attending
to more useful studies, or of following
more serious pursuits. They constituted

his amusement in many hours which
otherwise would have been unoccupied
and tedious. . . . The conversational
manner and discursive style were chosen
as best suited to the state of health of
the Author, who was incapable of considerable efforts and long-continued attention."

Any one who has read Sir Humphry
Davy's *Memoirs*, by his brother, John
Davy, M.D., F.R.S., will see that the
Salmonia is made up of his own experiences, and that the conversations between
Halieus, Poietes, Physicus, and Ornither
are reflections of his own varying moods,
when, in search of health, he wandered
alone among the glorious scenery of the
rivers he loved so well, both in this
country and on the Continent.* Many
of the passages in the *Salmonia* are transferred almost bodily from his *Journal*, with
the omission of those constant references
to his bodily sufferings with which his
Journal abounds. "How," he says, in
one entry, "I shall enjoy these glorious
mountains! But I have a furred tongue

* "Halieus" is supposed to be an accomplished
fly-fisher; "Ornither" is a gentleman generally
fond of the sports of the field; "Poietes is an
enthusiastic lover of nature; and "Physicus" is
the philosopher.

5

and a pulse at ninety-six. . . . I know not what my fate will be." In another pathetic entry he says : "*Dubito fortissime restaurationem meum,* as I have so often alluded to the possibility of my dying suddenly, I think it right to mention that I am too intense a believer in the Supreme Intelligence, and have too strong a faith in the optimism of the system of the universe, ever to accelerate my dissolution. The laurel water, therefore, which I have carried about with me, and used constantly, and from which I have decidedly derived benefit, is a prescription of Tomasini's ; and the laudanum and opium which are in my dressing-case, but which *I have never used,* were recommended to me in small doses to remove irritation, taken with purgatives. I have been, and am, taking a care of my health, which, I fear, it is not worth ; but which, hoping it may please Providence to preserve me for wise purposes, I think my duty."

His reference to "duty" reminds me that, in his *Salmonia,* Sir Humphry says : "Nelson was a good fly-fisher, and, as a proof of his passion for it, continued the pursuit even with his left hand. I have known a person who fished with him at Merton, in the Wandle. I hope this circumstance will be mentioned in the next edition of that most exquisite and touching Life of our hero by the Laureate,* an immortal monument raised by Genius to Valour."

Although I venture to think the form in which the *Salmonia* is cast, that of imaginary conversations, is not so successful in the hands of Sir Humphry as in those of his acknowledged prototype, Walton, just as Cotton is behind his master in the same style, still it is not certainly freshness of heart that the *Salmonia* lacks. What it does lack, it seems to me, is just that "genius" which, as I shall show further on, a great American writer, James Russell Lowell, denies to Walton. He might as well have denied it to Bunyan ; for if *The Compleat Angler* and *The Pilgrim's Progress* lack genius, whatever that may be, how can one account for the ever-increasing love of them, as generation after generation of men passes away?

To return to "J. D." and his *Secrets of Angling,* probably the best account of it will be found, as I have already noted, in the late Mr. T. Westwood's

* Southey. In Nelson's letters are to be found frequent references to the fish and fishing at Merton.—R. B. M.

"Introduction" to his edition of the work, certainly one of the best reprints we possess, inasmuch as it is "a strictly faithful and literal transcript of the edition of 1613."

Another pretty little reprint was published by E. and G. Goldsmid, of Edinburgh, in 1885. It was edited by "Piscator," who added some useful notes. Who "Piscator" is I do not know, but we are indebted to him also for the charming reprint of the *Treatyse* of Dame Juliana Berners, to which I have already referred. Of Mr. Arber's reprint in his *English Garner* Mr. Westwood speaks somewhat severely. "Mr. Arber," he says, " has thought it expedient to make many changes in the poem, and to introduce into it frequent supposed emendations. . . . He has altered the punctuation throughout, and modernised both the orthography and the syntax, robbing the verse, thereby, of much of its ancient air and aspect." He adds: "How far we have a right so to interfere with poets who are no longer here to defend themselves and to protect their own—how far it is justifiable to submit them to our individual and arbitrary, not to say dogmatic judgment, is a question we do not take on ourselves to decide."

The title-page of the first edition runs thus :—

THE

SECRETS OF ANGLING.

TEACHING

THE CHOISEST TOOLES
BAYTES AND SEASONS, FOR THE
TAKING OF ANY FISH, IN POND OR RIVER :
PRACTISED AND FAMILIARLY OPENED
IN THREE BOOKES.

By J. D. ESQUIRE.

Printed at London, for Roger Jackson, and are to be sould at his Shop neere Fleet Street Conduit, 1613.

In comparing, as I have carefully done, *The Secrets of Angling* with *A Treatyse of Fysshynge wyth an Angle*, it is not evident, I think, that John Dennys knew Dame Juliana's work. In some respects the *Secrets* are not to be compared with the *Treatyse* for value of information given as regards, for instance, the best of all fish-

ing—fly-fishing. Dennys, who wrote at
least a hundred years after Dame Juliana,
seems to have known little or nothing
about fishing for salmon, trout, etc., with
an artificial fly. I say artificial because
he certainly refers to dibbing with a
natural fly in his directions for taking the
chub and trout. But Dame Juliana gives
us most excellent directions for the
making of artificial flies for the different
months. To her belongs the honour of
telling us first that the noble salmon may
be taken with a fly. She says :—

"Also ye may take hym but it is
seldom seen with a dubbe at such tyme
as when he lepith in lyke fourme and
manere as ye doo a trought or a
graylynge."

Again, value for value, Dame Juliana
is far ahead of Dennys as regards instructions for making rods, lines, hooks, floats,
etc.

But if Dennys is not so advanced as
one might expect in the practical details
of angling, he is far ahead of all other
English angling writers who have attempted
to describe the art in verse. In the first
line of his " first booke " he tells us

"Of Angling, and the Art thereof I sing."

And in the second verse we have this

charming invocation to the water nymphs
to lend their aid and power to his verse :—

"You *Nymphs* that in the Springs and Waters
    sweet,
Your dwelling have, of every Hill and Dale,
And oft amidst the meadows greene doe meet
To sport and play, and heare the *Nightingale*;
And in the Rivers fresh doe wash your feet,
While Prognes* sister tels her wofull tale :
    Such ayde and power unto my verses lend
    As may suffice this little worke to end."

Then follow directions as to the best
time of year to select and cut woods for
rods : of these he prefers the hazel.

"For not the brittle *Cane,* nor all the rest,
I like so well, though it be long and light,
Since that the Fish are frighted with the least
Aspect of any glittering thing, or white :
    Nor doth it by one halfe so well incline,
    As doth the plyant rod to save the line."

Anglers have ever been particular as
to the shape of hook they prefer—some
like a round bend, some an oval, some a
mixture of square and round, and other
variations of in-turned point, out-turned
point, side twist, or "sneck," etc. These
various shapes are named after the places
at which they were originally made;

* Procne's sister Philomela. Procne was
turned into a swallow and Philomela into a
nightingale.

hence we have "Limerick," "Kendal," "Carlisle," etc. It would probably puzzle a hook-maker to make one of Dennys' favourite "Pegasus" pattern, as thus described by him ;—

> "That Hooke I love that is in compasse round,
> Like to the print that *Pegasus* did make,
> With horned hoofe upon *Thessalian* ground ;
> From whence forthwith Pernasses spring out
>   brake.
> That doth in pleasant Waters so abound :
> And of the *Muses* oft the thirst doth slake,
>   Who on his fruitfull bankes doe sit and sing
>   That all the world of their sweet tunes doth
>   ring."

Our author continually cautions his reader against using any bright or white colours either in his tackle or his dress : even if you have to mend your rod, it should not be done with white thread. His excellent advice respecting the angler's dress has often been quoted :—

> "And let your garments Russet be or gray,
> Of colour darke, and hardest to descry :
> That with the Raine or weather will away,
> And least offend the fearefull Fishes eye."

After recounting the objections which "some youthfull Gallant" may advance against the art, and comparing the vanities of town enjoyments with those of the angler, he says :—

"I count it better pleasure to behold
　The goodlie compasse of the loftie Skye,
　And in the midst thereof like burning gold
　The flaming Chariot of the World's great eye ;
　The watry cloudes that in the ayre uprold
　With sundry kindes of painted collours flie :
　　And fayre Aurora lifting up her head,
　　And blushing rise from old Thitonus bed.

"The Hills and Mountains raised from the
　　Plaines,
　The Plaines extended levell with the ground,
　The ground divided into sundry vaines,
　The Plaines inclos'd with running rivers rounde,
　The Rivers making way through nature's
　　chaine
　With headlong course into the sea profounde :
　　The surging sea beneath the valleys low,
　　The valleys sweet, and lakes that lovely
　　　flowe.

"The lofty woods, the forrests wide and long,
　Adorned with leaves and branches fresh and
　　greene,
　In whose coole bow'rs the birds with chaunt-
　　ing song,
　Doe welcome with their quire the *summers*
　　Queene,
　The meadowes faire where *Flora's* guifts
　　among,
　　The silver skaled fish that softlie swimme,
　　Within the brookes and Cristall watry
　　　brimme.

"All these and many more of his creation,
　That made the heavens, the *Angler* oft doth
　　see,
　And takes therein no little delectation,
　To think how strange and wonderfull they be,

Framing thereof an inward contemplation,
To set his thoughts from other fancies free
 And whiles hee lookes on these with joyfull
  eye,
 His minde is rapt above the starry skye."

Following these delightful verses, full of the pure spirit of poetry, we have what I think is the finest part of his work—viz., a history of angling through the different ages :—

"But how this Art of Angling did beginne,
 And who the use thereof and practise found,
 How many times and ages since have bin,
 Wherein the sunne hath daily compast round,
 The circle that the signes twice sixe are in :
 And yeelded yearly comfort to the ground,
  It were too hard for me to bring about,
  Since *Ovid* wrote not all that story out."

A fine description follows of the Deluge of Deucalion, when only he and his wife Pyrrha were saved, who being themselves too old to replenish the world, they consult the Oracle of Themis, and were directed to repair the loss of mankind by throwing behind them the bones of their grand-mother :—

"For long before that fearful *Deluge* great,
 The universall Earth had overflowne ;
 A heavenly power there placed had her seate,
 And answeres gave of hidden things un-
  knowne.

Thither they went her favour to intreat,
Whose fame throughout that coast abroad was
    blowne,
  By her advice some way or meane to finde,
  How to renew the race of humane kind.

"Prostrate they fell upon the sacred ground,
  Kissing the stones, and shedding many a
    teare ;
And lowly bent their aged bodies downe
Unto the earth, with sad and heavy cheere ;
Praying the Saint with soft and dolefull sound
That she vouchsafe their humble suite to heare.
  The Goddesse heard, and bad them goe and
    take
  Their mothers bones, and throw behind their
    backe."

After being long perplexed as to the
meaning of "this Oracle obscure, and
darke of sense," and wondering

"How with so great a sinne they might dis-
  pense
Their Parents bones to cast and throw about,"

they leave the Temple and wander forth.

"And now beholding better every place,
  Each Hill and Dale, each River, Rock, and
    Tree ;
And muzing thereupon a little space,
  They thought the earth their mother well
    might be,
And that the stones that lay before their face,
To be her bones did nothing disagree :
  Wherefore to prove if it were false or true
  The scattered stones behind their backs they
    threw.

"Forthwith the stones (a wondrous thing to
    heare)
Began to move as they had life conceiv'd,
And waxed greater than at first they were;
And more and more the shape of man receiv'd,
Till every part most plainly did appeare,
That neither eye nor sense could be deceiv'd:
    They heard, they spake, they went, and
        walked too,
    As other living men are wont to doe.

"Thus was the earth replenished anew
    With people strange, sprung up with little
    paine,
Of whose increase the progenie that grew,
Did soone supply the empty world againe;
But now a greater care there did insue
How such a mightie number to maintaine,
    Since foode there was not any found,
    For that great flood had all destroyed and
    drownd."

INVENTION OF THE ART OF ANGLING.

The Age of Wood.

The art of angling was now invented
to save the newly created inhabitants of
the world :—

"Then did Deucalion first the Art invent
Of *Angling*, and his people taught the same;
And to the Woods and groves with them he
    went
Fit tooles to finde for this most needful game;
There from the trees the longest ryndes they
    rent,
Wherewith strong Lines they roughly twist and
    frame,

And of each crooke of hardest Bush and Brake,
They made them Hooks the hungry Fish to take."

Every angler has experienced the difficulty of catching fish without bait ; but old Deucalion was equal to the occasion. He knows the fish are there :—

" And to intice them to the eager bit,
    Dead frogs and flies of sundry sorts he tooke ;
    And snayles and wormes such as he found
        most fit,
    Wherein to hide the close and deadly hooke :
    And thus with practise and inventive wit,
    He found the means in every lake and brooke
        Such store of Fish to take with little paine.
        As did long time this people new sustaine."

Angling in the Age of Gold.

" In this rude sorte began this simple Art,
    And so remain'd in that first age of old,
    When *Saturne* did *Amaltheas* horne impart
    Unto the World, that then was all of Gold ;
    The Fish has yet had felt but little smart,
    And were to bite more eager, apt, and bold :
        And plentie still supplide the place againe
        Of woefull want, whereof we now complaine." *

* Anglers, like farmers, are good grumblers. We have seen in a previous chapter how Leonard Mascall laments the bad case into which angling had fallen in his day. Dennys does the same, and so it goes on down to our time. We all know many a *laudator temporis acti* among our angling friends.

" But when in time the feare and dread of man
Fell more and more on every living thing,
And all the creatures of the world began
To stand in awe of this usurping King,
Whose tyranny so farre extended than
That Earth and Seas it did in thraldome bring ;
   It was a worke of greater paine and skill,
   The Wary Fish in Lake or Brooke to kill."

Angling in the Age of Silver and Brass.

"So worse and worse two ages more did passe,
Yet still this Art more perfect daily grew,
For then the slender Rod invented was,
Of finer sort than former ages knew,
And Hookes were make of silver and of brasse,
And Lines of Hempe and Flax were framed
   new,
   And sundry baites experience found out more,
   Than elder Times did know or try before."

Angling in the Iron Age.

But at the last the Iron age drew neere,
Of all the rest the hardest, and most scant,
Then lines were made of Silke and subtile hayre,
And Rods of lightest Cane and Hazell plant,
And Hookes of hardest steele invented were,
That neither skill nor workmanship did want,
   And so this art did in the end attaine
   Unto that state where now it doth remaine."

And so we come to the end of the
" first booke " of Dennys' *Secrets of Angling*,
and to the end of the, to me, perhaps
most interesting part of it. The second
book is a description in verse of what

Dame Juliana had already given us more than a century earlier, and more completely: viz., a description of the various kinds of fresh-water fish; their seasons; how, when, and where to take them; the different "bayts" to be used, etc. The last verse of this book runs thus :—

> "Thus have I shew'd how Fish of divers kinde
> Best taken are, and how their bayts to know ;
> But *Phoebus* now beyond the westerne *Inde*,
> Beginneth to descend and draweth low,
> And well the weather serves and gentle winde
> Downe with the tide and pleasant streame to
>   row,
>   Unto some place where we may rest us in,
> Untill we shall another time begin."

DENNYS' "THIRD BOOKE."

In this we again leave the practical and less poetic side of angling, and find some charming pictures of the angler's recreation, and of the qualities which a good angler should possess, of which there are twelve, not the least of them being Patience.

" For there are times in which they will not bite."

And the angler is described in a charming metaphor as being at times like a vessel waiting for a favourable wind :—

> "And as a ship in safe and quiet roade
> Under some hill or harbour doth abide,

With all her fraight, her tackling, and her load
Attending still the winde and wished tide,
Which when it serves, no longer makes abode,
But forth into the watry deepe doth slide,
   And through the waves divides her fairest
     way
   Unto the place where she intends to stay.

"So must the angler be provided still,
Of divers tooles, and sundry baytes in store;
And all things else pertaining to his store ;
Which he shall get and lay up long before,
That when the weather frameth to his will,
He may be well appointed evermore
   To take fit time whan it is offered ever,
   For time in one estate abideth never."

Very charming and musical in Dennys' verses are the two last lines of each, forming, as they often do, a refrain or burden of the whole. Much as I should like to quote the whole of the twelve "qualities of an angler," I must, for want of space, confine myself to one or two. One might imagine that Dennys knew what it was to stalk a wary Test or Itchen trout on a bright day in June, to judge from the following verse describing his fifth quality :—

" The fifth good gift is low Humilitie,
As when a lyon coucheth for his pray
So must he stoope or kneele upon his Knee,
To save his line or put the weeds away,
Or lye along sometime if neede there be,
For any let or chance that happen may,
   And not to scorne to take a little paine,
   To serve his turne his pleasure to obtaine."

I fear few modern anglers can lay much claim to possess the "eleventh gift of a good angler." Even Dennys called it the "hardest to endure"; but much depends on what he calls "superfluous fare":—

"The eleventh good gift and hardest to indure,
 Is fasting long from all superfluous fare,
 Unto the which he must himself inure,
 By exercise and use of dyet spare,
 And with the liquor of the waters pure,
 Acquaint himselfe if he cannot forbeare,
  And never on his greedy belly thinke
  From rising sunne untill a low he sincke."

With one more quotation from these *Secrets* I must leave Dennys: it is his last verse :—

"And now we are arrived at the last,
 In wished harbour where we meane to rest;
 And make an end of this our journey past ;
 Here then in quiet roade I thinke it best
 We strike our sailes and stedfast Anchor cast,
 For now the Sunne low setteth in the West,
  And yee Boat-Swaines, a merry *Carroll* sing
  To him that safely did us hither bring."

CHAPTER VI.

Gervase Markham's *Art of Angling* (1614) and other Books—His Work not merely a Prose Version of *The Secrets of Angling*—William Lawson, a North-Country Angler and Writer —*Barker's Delight*—Thomas Barker, a First-rate Trout-Fisher—Walton's Indebtedness to Him—The First Writer to Describe the Use of the Reel or Winch and the Gaff in Salmon-Fishing—His Directions for Fly-Making and Fly-Fishing.

ENNYS' own work, as originally printed in verse, is one of the rarest books in the English language ; but this did not detract from its value as a text-book, inasmuch as it was reprinted as a poem several times, and, in part, in prose editions under other titles, chiefly in connection with the works of that interesting and prolific writer and compiler Gervase Markham.

The original poem was first published in 1613, and it is curious to note that what the editors of the *Bibliotheca Pisca-*

toria call a " prose version " of it appeared
next year in the second part of *The
English Husbandman, drawne in Two
Books*, by Gervase Markham. I have in
my possession original copies of several
of Markham's books, including a fine
example of the 1631 thick quarto edition,
which contains most of them under the
general title *A Way to get Wealth*, in six
books. "I. Cheape and Good Husbandry. II. Country Contentments, including
Hunting, Hawking, Coursing with Grey-
hounds, Shooting in Longbow * or Cross-
bow, Bowling, Tennis, Baloone, THE
WHOLE ART OF ANGLING, the use of
the Fighting Cock. III. The English
Housewife, ' containing the Inward and
Outward Vertues which ought to be in
a Compleate Woman.' IV. The Enrich-
ment of the Weald of Kent. V. Markham's Farewell to Husbandry. VI. A
new Orchard and Garden, including the
Husbandry of Bees." Of these six books
it is said, " The first five Bookes gathered

---

* Archers might well wish that he had devoted
a good deal more space to a description of this
fascinating exercise. By the way, he says the
bow-string should be drawn by holding it with
the thumb as well as the fingers. As far as I
know, no other writer on archery recommends
the use of the thumb.—R. B. M.

by Gervase Markham, the last by William Lawson."

This most delightful old book, with its quaint woodcuts, has given me many an hour's enjoyment. Part VI., by William Lawson, should be read by every lover of orchards, bees, and gardens.

I am not aware that it has been previously pointed out that "The Whole Art of Angling" contained in this volume is not exactly what the editors of the *Bibliotheca Piscatoria* call it—viz., a prose version of *The Secrets of Angling*. Thanks again to my angling friend, Mr. W. B. Adlington, who was fortunate enough to pick it up at a second-hand bookseller's shop for the price "of an old song," I have been able to examine a copy of the first edition of his " prose version," which, as I have already stated, was published in 1614 with Markham's *Pleasures of Princes*. This very perfect and beautifully printed black-letter edition contains " A Discourse of the generall Art of Fishing with the Angle, or otherwise, and of all the hidden secrets belonging thereunto," together "with the Choyce, Ordering, Breeding, and Dyetting of the fighting Cocke."

It is pretty clear to me that this prose work on angling of 1614 was compiled by Markham, or by Lawson for Markham, from, not merely the *Secrets*, but also from the *Treatyse* and from Leonard Mascall—probably from Mascall and Dennys. Take, for instance, from the directions for making artificial flies one example,—and many a dish of fine trout have I killed in Yorkshire with the fly described.

DAME JULIANA BERNERS, 1496.

The Stone Fly.—"The Stone flye, the bodye of blacke wull ; and yellow under the wynge, and under the tayle and the wynges of the drake."

LEONARD MASCALL, 1590.

The Stone Fly.—"The body is made of blacke wooll, made yellow under the wynges and under the tayl, and so made with the winges of the drake."

GERVASE MARKHAM: "THE ART OF ANGLING," 1614.

"The Stone fly is made of blacke woll, made yellow under the wings, and under the tayle with silke, and the wings of drakes downe."

I think Dame Juliana's claim to be the first to give a dressing of this most deadly fly will not be disputed. Of course as time went on anglers improved in their imitations, and we find in Markham's book, in 1614, the advantages of cork as a material for fly-dressing recommended :—

"Now for the making of these flyes, the cloudie darke flye is made of blacke wool, clipt from between a sheepes ears, and whipt about with black silke, his wings of the under mayle of the Mallard, and his head made blacke and sutable, fixed upon a fine piece of cork, and folded so cunningly about the hooke, that nothing may be perceived but the point and beard onely."

These directions are not particularly clear, but it looks as if the foundation of the body was to be cork.

Here is a bit which will interest fly-fishers from *The Art of Angling* :—

"Now for the shapes and proportions of these flyes, it is impossible to describe them without paynting, therefore you shall take of these severall flyes alive, and laying them before you, trie how near your Art can come unto nature by an equall shapes and mixture of colours ; and when you have made them, you may keep them in close boxes uncrushed, and they will serve you many yeares."

As I have already said, this work can

hardly be called a prose version of the *Secrets* ; it consists of two or three only of the chapters of that work, with some from Leonard Mascall's book, and a few additions given apparently from the practical experience of the compiler.

WILLIAM LAWSON, ANGLER AND WRITER.

It is uncertain who made this compila tion in 1614, whether Markham himself or Lawson for him ; but about 1620 a second edition of the *Secrets* in verse, with notes by William Lawson, appeared, and in the complete edition of Markham's *Cheape and Goode Husbandry*, published in 1631, called on the title-page "Fifth Edition," we find the sixth book, "On the Orchard, Garden, Bees, etc.," is by William Lawson. In his dedication to Sir Henry Belosses, Lawson mentions his " 48 yeeres (and moe) experience in the North of England," so that he was probably a North-countryman. His very practical additions to the *Secrets*, and his " approved experiments," show clearly that he was an angler accustomed to fishing clear North-country streams. The following remark of his reminds one of Cotton's criticism of " southern " tackle :—

" I utterly dislike your southern corks.
First for they affright the fish, in the bite
and sight, and because they follow not so
kindly the nimble rod and hand. Secondly
they breed weight to the line, which puts
it in danger, and hinders the nimble jerk
of the rod, and loades the arm. A good
eye and hand may easily discern the bite."

He tells us that he makes his own
hooks out of the best Spanish and Millan
needles, and gives excellent illustrated
instructions in the manufacture. With
reference to a line in the *Secrets*, in which
Dennys says of the hook,

"His point not over sharp, not yet too dull,"

Lawson says truly, " He meanes the hooke
may be too weake at the point, it cannot
be too sharpe if the metal be good steele."

Lawson, as far as I know, was the first
angling writer to mention that fish of the
carp family have throat teeth.

" THE CAST OF THE FLIE."

Of the trout he remarks :—
" The trout makes the angler most
gentlemanly, and readiest sport of all
other fishes : if you angle with a made
fly, and a line twice your rod's length or
more (in a plaine water without wood)

of three haires, in a darke windy day
from afternoone, and have learned the
cast of the flie,* your flie must counterfeit
the may flie, which is bred of the cod-bait,
and is called the water-flie : you must
change his colour every month, beginning
with a dark white, and so grow to a
yellow, the forme cannot so well be put
on a paper, as it may be taught by slight "
. . . [Then follows a rough illustration in
which the setæ are represented in a curious
manner.]

"The head is of black silk or haire,
the wings of a feather of a mallard, teele,
or pickled-hen wing. The body of Crewell
according to the moneth for colour, and
run about with a black haire ; all fastened
at the taile with the thread that fastened
the hook. You must fish in, or hard by
the stream, and have a quick hand, and
a ready eye, and a nimble rod, strike with
him, or you lose him " (*i.e.*, strike at the
rise). "If the wind be rough, and trouble
the crust of the water, he will take it in
the plaine deeps, and then and there
commonly the greatest will rise. When
you have hookt him, give him leave,
keeping your line straight, and hold him

* I believe this is the first time in our angling
literature this expression is used, "the cast of
the flie."—R. B. M.

from roots, and he will tire himself. This is the chief pleasure of angling. This flie and two linkes among wood, or close by a bush, moved in the crust of the water, is deadly in an evening, if you come close. This is called bushing for trouts."

When this description of fly-fishing for trout with the May-fly was first published is doubtful. The only edition of the *Secrets* with Lawson's notes which I possess is that of Sir Henry Ellis, 1811, reprinted from the edition of 1652 (Walton's first edition appeared next year); but there was a previous edition in 1630, and one before that, "circa 1620," according to the *Bibliotheca Piscatoria*. At any rate to Lawson belongs the credit of the best description of fly-fishing for trout previous to Barker, Walton, and Cotton.

Of "divers wayes to catch the wrinkling eele," he gives very practical directions; in fact, I think Lawson is much more deserving of a place in that Valhalla of angling writers the *Bibliotheca Piscatoria* than some who figure therein. It will be seen by the following extract that he got in, as it were, only by the skin of his teeth :—

"Lawson (William). *A new Orchard and Garden*, etc. London, 1617-8, 1626, etc., 4to.

' (Admissible, by stress of courtesy, and for the sake of that ' pleasant River with silver streams' that the old writer would fain have in his orchard, and wherein he might 'angle a freckled trout, sleighty eel, or some other dainty Fish')."

"BARKER'S DELIGHT."

Between Lawson and Walton came a quaint and very original little work, *Barker's Delight.* Old Barker was evidently a first-rate trout-fisher, and his book has special interest for the fly-fisher,[*] for reasons which I shall presently mention. If Barker had called his work *Barker's Angling*, or, as he might appropriately enough have done, *Barker's Trout-Fishing*, it would have attracted much more attention than it has received. An author never makes a greater mistake than when he uses as the leading title of his book some phrase or expression or word which conveys no idea of the contents. It does not matter how full the

---

[*] Here is a hint from Barker which may be of assistance to some amateur maker of fishing-flies for dry-fly fishing :—

" Once more, my good brother, I'll speak in thy
      ear ;
  Hog's, red cow's, and bear's wool, to float best
      appear."

second title may be; hundreds for whom it is intended miss it, passing over the large-type leading title which conveys nothing. Such an ambiguous title, especially when it has no explanatory sub-title, is the bane of the compiler of catalogues, and frequently robs the author of much of the credit to which he is entitled.

Walton freely acknowledges his indebtedness to Barker. When Piscator and Viator are sitting smoking in the shade of the sycamore tree after breakfast, Viator reminds his master of his "promised direction for making and ordering my artificial flye," and to this replies :—

Piscator. "My honest Scholar, I will do it, for it is a debt due unto you, by my promise : and because you shall not think your self more engaged* to me than indeed you really are, therefore I will tell you freely. I find Mr. Thomas Barker (a Gentleman that has spent much time and money in angling) deal so judicially and freely in a little book of his of Angling, and especially of making and angling with a flye for a Trout, *that I will give you his very directions without much variation,* which shall follow."

* Indebted.

I find that, in his "much corrected
and enlarged Fifth Edition," Walton says
(I quote from a copy of that edition in
my possession) : " I shall next give you
some other Directions for Flie-fishing,
such as are given by Mr. Thomas Barker,
a gentleman that hath spent much time
in Fishing : *but I shall do it with a little
variation."*

Of Thomas Barker we have some information scattered here and there in his
pages. I have before me a charming
little reprint given me some years ago by
the editor, Mr. C. S. Bentley, F.S.A., of
the Gresham Angling Society. Barker
tells us that he was born and educated
at " Bracemeale in the Liberty of Salop,
being a Freeman and Burgesse of the
same City." Bracemeal or Brace-meole
is a parish in Shrewsbury district, Salop,
one mile south of Shrewsbury,* on the
river Severn, still one of our finest
salmon rivers. Doubtless Barker gained
his experience of salmon-fishing on that
river ; for he is the first writer who
writes apparently from actual experience
of salmon-fishing, and in those delightful
tributaries of the Severn he would have
full scope for that fly-fishing for trout

---

* *Imperial Gazetteer.*

which he knew and loved so well. He speaks in his "Epistle Dedicatory," in his enlarged second edition, published in 1657, of having been threescore years gathering the information, so that he was probably a young man when Walton was born. It is most likely that he was acquainted with Walton, for this second edition was published by Walton's publisher, Richard Marriot, and in it he tells us that "I live in Henry the 7ths Gifts, the next door to the Gatehouse in Westminster," and offers to give information about fishing to "any noble or gentle Angler" who may desire it.

In addition to having the honour of providing Walton with much of his information in the highest branch of angling, fly-fishing, and giving the first clear but simple directions for fly-making, Barker, so far as I have been able to trace, was the first English writer to mention the use of the winch.

BARKER THE FIRST TO DESCRIBE THE USE OF THE REEL OR WINCH AND THE GAFF IN ANGLING FOR SALMON OR OTHER FISH.

Not long since I saw a statement in an angling paper that the use of the winch was not mentioned by Walton. This is both true and not true ; it is not mentioned in his first edition, but in others it is.

Page 146, fifth edition, *Compleat Angler* : " Note also, that many use to fish for a salmon with a ring of wire on the top of their Rod, through which the Line may run to as great a length as is needful when he is hook'd. And to that end, some use a wheel about the middle of their rod, or near their hand, which is to be observed better by seeing one of them, than by a large demonstration of words."

But Barker, who wrote before Walton, not only describes the reel, but gives an illustration of it. This passage is very interesting. He says (p. 18) :—

" I will now shew you the way to take *Salmon.* The first thing you must gain must be a rod of some ten foot in the stock that will carry a top of six foot pretty stiffe and strong, the reason is, because there must be a little wire ring at the upper end of the top for the line to run through, that you may take up and loose the line at your pleasure ; you must have your winder within two foot of the bottom to goe on your rod made in this manner, with a spring, that you may put it as low as you please."

(Compare this with the extract just

previously given, and it will be clear where Walton got his description of the reel from, though Barker knew too much about it to say it is put on the middle of the rod.)

Barker continues :—

" The Salmon swimmeth most commonly in the midst of the river. In all his travells his desire is to see the uppermost part of the river, travelling on his journey in the heat of the day he may take a bush [*i.e.,* rest in the shade of a bush]; if the fisherman espy him, he goeth at him with his speare, so shorteneth his journey.

" The angler that goeth to catch him with a line and hook, must angle for him as nigh the middle of the water as he can with one of these baits : He must take two lob-worms baited as handsomely as he can, that the four ends may hang meet [evenly] of a length, and so angle as nigh the bottom as he can, feeling your plummet to run on the ground some twelve inches from the hook : if you angle for him with a flie (which he will rise at like a trout) the flie must be made of a large hook, which hook must carry six wings, or four at least ; there is judgment in making these flyes. The Salmon will come at a Gudgeon in the manner of a trouling, and

cometh at it bravely, which is fine angling
for him and good. You must be sure
that you have your line of twenty-six yards
of length, that you may have your convenient time to turne him, or else you
are in danger to lose him : but if you turn
him you are very like to have the fish
with small tackles : the danger is all in
the running out both of Salmon and Trout,
you must forecast to turn the fish as you
do a wild horse, either upon the right or
left hand, and wind up your line as you
finde occasion in the guiding of the fish
to shore, *having a good large landing hook
to take him up.*"

The words italicised are the earliest
reference to the use of the gaff which
I have noticed in an angling writer. It
was not till long after Walton's time that
the use of the reel became general.

Barker was also the first writer to divide
artificial flies into the two great divisions
of—

1. Palmer, hackle, or spider-dressed
flies.

2. Winged flies.

He says (p. 32) : " Now I will shew you
how to make flies. Learn to make two
flies and make all, that is, the Palmer
ribbed with gold or silver, and the May-
flye. These are the ground [or founda-

7

tion] of all flyes." He then gives the best
and simplest description of how to make
artificial flies then extant; it is used in
full by Walton, and until Cotton's work
appeared may truly be termed "the fly-
fisher's text-book." Indeed, the more
Barker's book is considered from the
angler's point of view, the more it im-
presses itself on one as the work of a
thoroughly practical angler, who was in
many respects far ahead of his time.
Take, for instance, this specimen of his
writing :—

" My Lord sent me at Sun going down
to provide him a good dish of trouts
against the next morning by sixe of the
clock. I went to the door to see how the
wanes of the air were like to prove. I
returned answer, that I doubted not, God
willing, but to be provided at his time
appointed. I went presently to the river,
and it proved very dark, I drew out a
line of three silks and three hairs twisted
for the uppermost part, and a line of two
hairs and two silks twisted for the lower
part, with a good large hook : I baited my
hook with two lob-worms, the four ends
hanging as meet [even] as I could guess
them in the dark, I fell to angle. It
proved very dark, so that I had great sport
angling with the lob-worms as I doe with

the flye on the top of the water: you
shall heer the fish rise at the top of the
water, then you must loose a slack line
down to the bottom as nigh as you can
guess, then hold your line strait, feeling
the fish bite, give time, there is no doubt
of losing the fish, for there is not one
among twenty but doth gorge the bait;
the least stroke you can strike fastens the
hook and makes the fish sure; letting
the fish take a turn or two, you may
take the fish up with your hands. The
night began to alter and grow somewhat
lighter, I took off the lob-worm and set
to my rod a white Palmer-flye, made of
a large hook; I had sport for the time
until it grew lighter, so I took off the
white Palmer and set to a Red Palmer
made of a large hook; I had good sport
until it grew very light. Then I took
off the Red Palmer and set to a Black
Palmer; I had good sport, made up the
dish of fish. So I put up my tackles and
was with my Lord at the time appointed
for the service.

"'These three flies with the help of
the lob-worms serve to angle all the year
for the night, observing the times as I
have shewed you in this night-work, the
white flye for darknesse, the red flye in
medio, and the black flye for lightnesse.

This is the true experience for angling in the night, which is the surest angling of all, and killeth the greatest Trouts."

Although old Barker was fishing for his master's breakfast, there is the right ring about his writing. Many a lusty ancestor must he have slain of those admirable fellows of Shropshire, Yorkshire, and most other English shires some of us have had more than a passing acquaintance with.

Not alone was Walton indebted to Barker. Colonel Venables took his *Night Angling* for trout straight from Barker. I wonder if they ever met and smoked a pipe together—Barker, Walton, and Venables? Richard Marriot published for all of them, and surely they must all have met at his shop in St. Dunstan's Churchyard, Fleet Street.

Barker not only knew how to kill trout, but also how to cook them, and much of his little volume is taken up with instructions of a culinary nature. And uncommonly good they appear to be: take this one example (p. 13): he says :—

"BROYLED TROUTS.

"We must have one dish of Broyled Trouts, when the intrails be taken out, you must cut them across the side : being

washed clean, you must take some sweet
herbs, as thyme, sweet marjoram, and
parsley chopped very small, the trouts
being cut somewhat thick, and fill the
cuts full with the chopt herbs, then make
your gridiron fit to put them on, being
well cooled with rough suet, then lay
the Trouts on a charcoal fire : as you turn
them baste them with fresh butter untill
you think they are well broyled, the
sauce must be butter and vinegar, the
yolk of an egge beaten, beat all together
and put it on the fish for the service."

" The best Trouler for a Pike in England.

" There was one of my name," says
Barker, " the best trouler for a Pike within
this Realm of England ; the manner of
his trouling was with a hasell rod some
twelve foot long, with a ring of wire in
the top of the rod for his line to run
through : within two feet of the bottom
of the rod there was a hole made to put
in a winder to turn with a barrell, to
gather up his line and loose it at his
pleasure. This was his manner of
trouling with a small fish."

And here I will leave this famous old
angler and cook, whose little book was

first published in 1651, giving a copy of
the title-page of his second edition :—

BARKER'S DELIGHT,

OR

THE ART OF

ANGLING.

WHEREIN ARE DISCOVERED MANY RARE
SECRETS VERY NECESSARY TO BE
KNOWN BY ALL THAT DELIGHT
IN THAT RECREATION, BOTH
FOR CATCHING THE FISH,
AND DRESSING
THEREOF.

The Second Edition much enlarged.

By THOMAS BARKER,

AN ANTIENT PRACTITIONER IN THE SAID ART.

Eccles. iii. 1, 11.
"There is a time and season to every purpose under
Heaven ; Everything is beautifull in his time."

London : printed by J. G. for Richard Marriot,
and sold at his shop in S. Dunstan's Church-
yard, Fleet Street, 1657.

CHAPTER VII.

Walton and the World's Fair, 1893—A Glance at the Times in which He Lived—Some Account of the Chief Particulars of Walton's Life which have Come Down to Us—No Proof Exists that He was ever a "Sempster, Haberdasher, or Hamburgh Merchant"— His Connection with the Ironmongers' Company—His First Marriage—Offices Held by Him in the Parish of St. Dunstan's-in-the West—Loss of His First Wife and Seven Children during His Residence in Chancery Lane—His Second Marriage—His Connections by Marriage with the Cranmer and Ken Families—Birth of His Son Isaac— Was Probably Residing in Clerkenwell when His *Compleat Angler* was First Published—Walton a Staunch Royalist—Incident After the Battle of Worcester—Death of His Second Wife—Lives at the Houses of Dr. Morley, Bishop of Winchester, and Dr. Ward, Bishop of Salisbury—Dies at Winchester, December 15th, 1683.

THE other day I had the following letter from an American friend, Dr. James A. Henshall, author of *The Book of the Black Bass*, who has charge of the Angling

Department of the great "World's Fair" at Chicago :—

"World's Columbian Commission.   Office of the
"Director-General of the Exposition.
"CHICAGO, ILL., U.S.A., *March 27th*, 1893.

"DEAR MR. MARSTON,—There will be a reproduction of Walton and Cotton's fishing-house on the World's Fair grounds to celebrate the 300th anniversary of Izaak Walton's birthday, which occurs August 9th, 1893.

"I would very much like a good photograph of his statue in Winchester Cathedral, in order to have an enlarged print made from it to place in the house.   If you can procure a good one, and will mail it to me, I shall be very much gratified, and will cheerfully re-pay you for any expense that you may incur.   The fine illustrations of the house in your 'Centennial Edition' will prove of great assistance in the reproduction of the structure.

"With kindest regards, and in the hope of seeing you this summer,

"I am, yours very truly,
"J. A. HENSHALL,

"In charge Angling Pavilion, Fisheries
"Building, Jackson Park, Chicago.

"MR. R. B. MARSTON,
"Editor *Fishing Gazette*, London, England."

I of course gladly sent the photograph of the statue, and also others of the fishing-house, of which Cotton says, writing in March 1676: "My house stands upon the margin of one of the finest rivers for Trouts and grayling in England. . . . I have lately built a little Fishing House upon it, dedicated to Anglers, over the door of which you will see the two first Letters of my Father Walton's name and mine twisted in Cypher as in the title page."

It is certainly pleasing to think that in this greatest of all great world's fairs there is place for and thought for the old angler and biographer. "Red Spinner," who has given us such vivid pictures of the Fair in the columns of *The Daily News*, describes the general effect as "overwhelming." Pleasant will it be then for the angler to come across this little oasis dedicated to Walton, or, in other words, to peace, contentment, and the love of quiet country life.

But Walton is not out of place at Chicago. Extremes meet; and we have, as it were, a precedent for it in the contrast between Walton's calm life and the turbulent, terrible times in which he lived. As I said in my edition of his work: "It has often appeared strange to me, when reading a chapter or two of *The Compleat Angler*, that these delightful pictures of the 'contemplative man's recreation,' these charming scenes of peaceful, pastoral life, should have been produced by a man who had lived through the horrors of the Civil Wars—sieges, battles, skirmishes, and countless struggles between the Royalist and Parliamentarian forces, in which brother often fought against brother and father against son."

WALTON ON HIS OWN TIMES.

In his admirable Lives Walton gives some stirring pictures of the times in which he lived. In his Life of Dr. Robert Sanderson he says :—

"Some years before the unhappy Long Parliament, this nation being then happy and in peace, (though inwardly sick of being well,) namely in the year 1639, a discontented party of the Scots Church were zealously restless for another reformation of their Kirk-government; and to that end created a new covenant. . . . The Presbyterian party of this nation did again, in the year 1643, invite the Scotch covenanters back into England: and hither they came marching with it [the covenant] gloriously upon their pikes and on their hats, with this motto : ' For the Crown and Covenant of both Kingdoms.' This I saw, and suffered by it.

" But when I look back upon the ruin of families, the bloodshed, the decay of common honesty, and how the former piety and plain-dealing of this now sinful nation is turned into cruelty and cunning, I praise God that he prevented me from being of that party which helped to bring in this covenant, and those sad confusions that have followed it." *

A Brief Biographical Notice of Walton.

Izaak Walton was born on August 9th, 1593, in the parish of St. Mary in the town of Stafford. Of his father, Jervis

* The following extract, from a list, published in 1647, of the names of officers under command of General Sir Thomas Fairfax, is a grim commentary on Walton's lament: "Major Cook, died before Bristol; Lieutenant-Colonel Frances, slain at Naseby; Lieutenant-Colonel Cottesworth, slain before Oxford; Captain Hill, slain before Bristol; Captain Wilks, slain at Basing; Colonel Lloyd, slain at Taunton; Captain Wigsal, slain at Berkeley Castle; Captain Jenkins, slain at Farringdon, succeeded by Captain Tompkins, slain at Naseby; Lieutenant-Colonel Ingoldesby, slain at Pendennis; Major Cromwell, slain at Bristol," etc., etc. Our ancestors meant business when they fought; at Edgehill they killed about three thousand of each other, or six thousand in one day—a tremendous proportion of the small armies engaged.

Walton, little is known; he died about
three years after Walton was born. Of
his mother not even the name has been
discovered, and it is doubtful whether
she survived her husband. There appears
to be no proof whatever for Dr. Zouch's
statement in his Life of Walton that
his mother was the daughter of Edmund
Cranmer, Archdeacon of Canterbury.

Walton received a fair education, probably at the Grammar School of his
native town; and though there is no
record of his life from the date of his
baptism until we find him in London in
1618, it is fair to infer that his first
angling experiences were probably as a
youngster at Stafford, wandering with
some congenial spirit along the banks of
the neighbouring streams, armed with
hazel rod and horse-hair line.

Sir Harris Nicolas says the first reference to Walton when a young man is
in the dedication of a short poem entitled
The Love of Amos and Laura, by S. P.,*
published in 1619 (the year before *The
Mayflower* sailed for New England), to
which attention was first drawn by T.
Payne Collier in *The Poetical Decameron*,
vol. ii., p. 111.

A fact which seems to have escaped

* Samuel Purchas.

the notice of that most careful and in
defatigable of all Walton's biographers,
Sir Harris Nicolas, appears to me to
prove that Walton came to London prior
to 1613, the earliest date mentioned by
Sir Harris. The records of the Ironmongers' Company show that on November 12th, 1618, Walton, who is described
as *late apprentice to Mr. Thomas Grinsell*,
was made a member of that company.
This would seem to indicate that
Walton began life in London as an
apprentice when he was about sixteen
years of age—*i.e.*, about the year 1611.
The statement of Sir John Hawkins that
Walton's first settlement in London as a
shopkeeper was in the Royal Burse in
Cornhill, built by Sir Thomas Gresham,
in 1616, is not supported by proof of any
kind; nor is there any evidence to show
that he was ever a sempster, haberdasher,
or Hamburgh merchant, as stated by most
of his biographers, while there is direct
evidence that he was engaged in a
totally different business.

The records of the Ironmongers' Company, as already mentioned, prove that he
was made a member of that company on
November 12th, 1618. It does not follow
as a matter of course that Walton was
an ironmonger by trade because he was

a member of the Ironmongers' Company ; but in his marriage licence with Rachel Floud, dated· December 27th, 1626, he is described as of the " Cittie of London, Ironmonger." Surely, if he had been a sempster or haberdasher, he would not have called himself an ironmonger ?

"No circumstance," says Mr. Nicholl, F.S.A., in his *History of the Ironmongers' Company*, "has given me more gratification than the discovery that Izaak Walton is enrolled among their members." The records of the company give other interesting facts about Walton. We find that "he served as a gentleman in foins in the mayoralty of Sir Thomas Campbell in 1629, and performed the like service in 1635, in the pageant provided for Sir Christopher Clitherow."

In 1637 Walton was chosen Warden of the Yeomanry, and in 1639 paid over to his successor the sum of £2 7s. 10d., the balance left in his hands after discharging the duties of that office. He is again mentioned in 1641, the Lord Mayor having addressed three several precepts to the city companies,—requiring them, in the first place, to make a return of all their members, with their several places of abode ; secondly, to collect the moneys rated upon them respectively by Act of

Parliament; and, lastly, to signify that the sum of £40,000 was immediately required for the important affairs of the kingdom. Whereupon the Ironmongers were severally assessed for this purpose, and Walton appears in the list of Yeomanry, and is there described as "Isaacke Walton of the Parish of St. Dunstan's in the West," his contribution amounting to the sum of £3.

Beyond this we find no further mention of him in the Records, except in an account of arrears of quarterage. From this it may be inferred that his residence was not then known to the officers of the company.

On December 27th, 1626, Walton was married to Rachel Floud in the parish church of St. Mildred at Canterbury. Respecting his first residence in London, Sir John Hawkins states, on the authority of a deed in his possession, that in 1624 "Walton dwelt on the north side of Fleet Street, in a house two doors west of the end of Chancery Lane, and abutting on a messuage known by the sign of the *Harrow*," and that this house was then in the joint occupation of himself and a hosier called John Mason. It appears from the parish books of St. Dunstan's that from 1628 to 1644 his residence was in Chancery Lane, "about

the seventh house on the left-hand side,"
that he filled a parish office in December
1632; served on the jury in 1633; was
appointed a constable on December 20th,
1636; was again on the grand jury in 1638;
was one of the overseers of the poor in
and a sidesman on April 18th, 1639; and
a vestryman in February 1640. He continued to reside in Chancery Lane until
about August 1644. He was appointed ex-
aminer of St. Dunstan's August 27th, 1641,
was elected a vestryman in 1644; but at a
vestry holden on August 20th in the same
year another person was chosen "in the
room of Isaak Walton lately departed out
of this parish and dwelling elsewhere."

From 1644 to 1651 there is some
uncertainty as to where Walton lived.
Anthony Wood, the Oxford antiquary, tells
us that, "finding it dangerous for honest
men to be there, he left that city [London],
and lived sometimes at Stafford; but
mostly in the families of the eminent
clergymen of England, of whom he was
much beloved."

While making some inquiries at Stafford about Walton's connection with that
town, the most interesting relic I came
across was a note by him referring to
his house and land at Shallowford (of
which note I have given a facsimile copy

in my edition of the *Angler*). From this note, dated October 23rd, 1676, it appears that Walton bought the property in 1656, and had "had peaceable possession of it twenty-two years."

Walton's description and bequeathal of this property are given in his will. He left it to his son Izaak, and in the event, as happened, of his death without issue to the corporation of Stafford, "for the good and benefit of the said town."*

Hearing later from the Mayor of Stafford that he had been obliged to abandon the

---

* Proposed Memorial of Walton in London.

Since these lines were written the Mayor of Stafford has consulted me with respect to the celebration in this country of the tercentenary of Walton's birth. On a previous page I have referred to what they propose to do in America. He said that Mr. Andrew Lang had been asked to preside at a banquet, but was unable to accept, as he would be far away at the time. I suggested that we need not go far for a chairman. Seeing that it was Walton's birth at Stafford we wished to celebrate, what could be more appropriate than that the Mayor of Stafford should preside? And I was certain he would be well supported, especially if the affair took place in or near London. I also said that I had been thinking over the matter for some time, and it appeared to me that we ought to mark the occasion by something more permanent than a banquet; that, whereas the place of Walton's

8

idea of any celebration of the tercentenary at Stafford, it was decided to hold an informal celebration of the event at Broxbourne, on the Lea. Delegates from the principal London angling associations and other visitors were present at a pleasant gathering of disciples of Walton, presided over by Mr. William Senior, the angling editor of *The Field*. It was resolved that, as there was no memorial of Walton in London, funds should be raised to put a stained-glass window in St. Dunstan's, Fleet Street, with which church he was

birth and death had memorials of him, London, where he lived so long, where his children were born, and his *Angler* and other works published, had none. I added that I had written to the Rector of St. Dunstan's, Fleet Street, the Rev. William Martin, making the suggestion, and expressing the hope that he would approve of it. I have just received Mr. Martin's reply :—

"ST. DUNSTAN'S VESTRY, FLEET STREET, E.C.
"*June 12th*, 1893.

"MY DEAR MR. MARSTON,—I cordially approve of your suggestion, and I am very grateful to you for writing to me about it.

"I should consider it a great honour to St. Dunstan's Church to have some memorial in it of Izaak Walton. I had better see you about it when it is convenient to you.

"Very sincerely yours,
"WILLIAM MARTIN.

"R. B. MARSTON, Esq."

so long connected, and where so many
of those near and dear to him were buried.
The vicar, the Rev. W. Martin, tells me
that the cost of the window will only be
about £100, and I confidently hope we
shall not only obtain this, but also a handsome surplus for the funds of the Anglers'
Benevolent Society.

During Walton's residence in Chancery
Lane, he experienced severe afflictions by
the loss of no less than seven children,
besides his wife and her mother. Walton's
first wife, Rachel Floud, died on August
25th, 1640. About six years later he
married again, his second wife being Anne,
daughter of Thomas Ken, an attorney
in the Court of Common Pleas.

By his first marriage Walton became
connected with the Cranmer family, his
wife, Rachel Floud, being a daughter of
Susannah, daughter of Thomas Cranmer,
of Canterbury, son of Edmund Cranmer,
Archdeacon of Canterbury, and a grand
nephew of the great archbishop.

By his second marriage he became
connected with a family "united by alliance with several noble houses": his wife
was the half-sister of Thomas Ken, afterwards the deprived Bishop of Bath and
Wells. Walton was fifty-three at the time
of his second marriage, his wife being

about five-and-thirty ; he himself tells us,
in the inscription on her monument in
Worcester Cathedral, that she was "a
woman of remarkable prudence, and of
the primitive piety ; her great and general
knowledge being adorn'd with such true
humility, and blessed with soe much Chris-
tian meeknesse as made her worthy of
a more memorable monument." It is
certain, from these lines and others addressed to her by Walton, that their married
life of sixteen years was a very happy
one.   The first child of this marriage was
a daughter, Anne, born March 11th, 1648.
In 1650 a son was born, but only lived
a few months, making the eighth child
Walton lost by death.   In 1651, on
September 7th, another son was born,
the note of his birth being thus entered
by Walton in the family Prayer Book :—

"My last son Isaac, born the 7th of
September, 1651, at half an hour after two
o'clock in the afternoon, being Sunday,
and so was baptized in the evening by
Mr. Thornton in my house in Clerken-
well.   Mr. Henry Davison and Brother
Beauchamp were his God-fathers, and
Mrs. Row his God-mother."

From 1650 to 1661 Walton appears to
have resided at Clerkenwell.   It was
during his residence here that the first

edition of *The Compleat Angler* (1653) was published.

It was also during this period that occurred the incident of his being instrumental in preserving the lesser George which belonged to Charles II., as related by Ashmole in his history of the Order of the Garter.

Soon after the battle of Worcester, September 3rd, 1651, when Cromwell defeated the King with a loss of six thousand men and all their baggage, a collar of 🐍🐍,* and a garter which belonged to his majesty, formed part of the spoil, and were brought to Parliament a few days afterwards by Major Corbet, who was despatched by Cromwell with an account of his victory. The sovereign's lesser George was, however, preserved by Colonel Blague, who, having taken shelter at Blore Pipe House, two miles from Eccleshall, in Staffordshire, then the residence of Mr. George Barlow, delivered the jewel into that gentleman's custody. In the ensuing week Mr. Barlow carried it to

---

* In his charming little work *Hic et Ubique*, Sir William Fraser has this note : "Endless disputes have been held in relation to the collar of 🐍🐍. I presume to suggest that they are intended to indicate the word 'sanctissimus,' abbreviated."

Robert Milward, Esq., who was at that
time a prisoner in the garrison of Stafford,
and Milward shortly afterwards gave it
into "the trusty hands" of Mr. Izaak
Walton, to convey to Colonel Blague,
who was confined by the Parliament in
the Tower of London. It is said that
Colonel Blague, "considering it had
already passed so many dangers, was persuaded it could yet secure one hazardous
attempt of his own"; and having made his
escape from the Tower, he had the gratification of restoring the George to the
King.

Ashmole relates this interesting anecdote
from the statements of Blague, Milward,
and Walton, and speaks of the latter as "a
man well known, and as well beloved of
all good men, and will be better known
to posterity by his ingenious pen in the
Lives of Dr. Donne, Sir Henry Wotton,
Mr. Richard Hooker, and Mr. George
Herbert."

That the service Walton thus performed
for his King was one of great peril there
can be no doubt: he had to communicate
between two Royalist prisoners, through
a country full of Cromwell's rough soldiery
and adherents; he carried what might
have cost him his life, had it been discovered in his possession; for had not

Parliament proclaimed "that whoever shall assist the King with Horse, Arms, Plate or Money against them, are Traytors to the Parliament"?—and they had a short, sharp way of dealing with "Traytors."

Between 1651 and 1661 almost the only particulars we have of Walton are from scattered references in his works. He lost his second wife, Anne, in 1662, and in December of that year he obtained from his friend Gilbert Sheldon, Bishop of London, a lease of a newly erected building, adjoining a house called the Cross Keys, in Paternoster Row, for forty years, at the yearly rent of forty shillings, which premises were burnt in the Great Fire of London.

"After the Restoration" (1660), says Dr. Zouch, "Walton and his daughter had apartments constantly reserved for them in the houses of Dr. Morley, Bishop of Winchester, and Dr. Ward, Bishop of Salisbury."

The charming letter from Walton to Cotton which is prefixed to the first edition of Cotton's Part II. of *The Compleat Angler* is dated "London, 1676." I have just copied it from a little time-worn edition of that date now in my possession, which is bound up in the original old calf binding with the fifth

edition of Walton and Colonel Venables'
Experienc'd Angler. I must refer more
fully to this little volume presently.

Walton died at Winchester on December 15th, 1683, during the memorable
frost of that year, at the Prebendal House
of his son-in-law, Dr. Hawkins, whom, as
he says in his will, he loved as his own
son.   He was buried in Winchester
Cathedral, in Prior Silkstead's Chapel;
a large black marble slab in the floor of
the chapel marks his resting-place. "The
morning sun falls directly on it, reminding
the contemplative man of the mornings
when he was for so many years up and
abroad with his angle."

It was my good fortune to be able
to accomplish, by the assistance of the
readers of *The Fishing Gazette,* what had
for nearly a century been the wish of
admirers of Walton—viz., that a statue of
him should be erected to his memory in
Winchester Cathedral. The Very Rev.
Dr. Kitchin, Dean of Winchester, gave us
the kindest assistance, reserving a niche
in the beautiful great screen in the
cathedral for the statue, which was very
ably executed by Miss Mary Grant.

CHAPTER VIII.

The First Editions of *The Compleat Angler*—Effect on My Library of the Abnormally Early May-Fly Season of this Year (1893)—Curious Printer's Error in the Copies First Printed of the *Angler*—Walton's First Title-Page—His "Epistles Dedicatory" and "Addresses to the Reader"—Some Past and Present Money-Values of a First Edition.

 HAVE before me an original copy of the FIRST EDITION of Walton's book in a very perfect state of preservation. I have borrowed it from the "Amateur Angler," who, writing in *The Fishing Gazette* on May 12th, 1888, says, in an article called "An Outing with Izaak Walton on a Fine May Morning "* :—

"I am the happy possessor of a perfect copy of the first edition of *The Compleat Angler*. The title runs thus: *The Compleat Angler, or the Contemplative Man's Recreation*.

* Since reprinted with other articles under the title of *Days in Clover*."

"The above portion of the title-page is beautifully engraved on a scroll, with a pair of dolphins above and a pair below, and a bunch of fish pendent from the tails of the upper ones on either side of the scroll. Then follows in plain type : ' Being a discourse of Fish and Fishing, not unworthy the perusal of most anglers. [And between two rules] Simon Peter said, "I go a-fishing"; and they said, "We also will go with thee."—John xxi. 3. (London : Printed by T. Maxey, for RICH. MARRIOT, in St. Dunstan's Churchyard, Fleet-street, 1653.) '

"Izaak Walton's name does not appear on this title-page ; but in an advertisement of it in *The Perfect Diurnal*, it is said to be ' Of eighteen-pence price. Written by Iz. Wa.' It was published in the beginning of the month of May."

But this copy, although of the first edition, is not one of the first copies printed of that edition, as those contained a printer's error, which, when Walton discovered it, doubtless made him put on his hat, and go with all speed to his friend and publisher Richard Marriot to stop the press.

Since writing these lines I have had a rare hunt all over my library to find a copy of a reprint of the first edition

containing the error. The May-fly came
up all out of time this year. I had to hurry
off to Hampshire almost three weeks
earlier than usual. On my return I found
that a terrible thing had happened ; and
yet I was expected to say, and did say,
it was delightful. My library had been
"dusted and put straight." Goodness
knows it required it badly enough ! Still,
I groaned inwardly as my eyes wandered
in search of the old familiar landmarks.

It was as if an earthquake had taken
place, and the face of the country was all
altered. A few weeks ago I knew that
this particular edition of Walton was in
the latitude of White's *Selborne* and the
longitude of Landor's *Imaginary Conversations* ; but Landor I find has been
promoted, and White I have not yet
found. Books which for years have been
in the Northern Hemisphere are now new
islands in the South Pacific. I feel like
a sailor without compass or chart. Even
great continents have been split up.
Fourteen volumes of *The Literature of the
1883 Fisheries Exhibition* until recently
stood shoulder to shoulder ; now five of
them are missing—lost for the present in
the multitude. In this hot weather it
gives one a feeling of hopelessness. I
want one book. I must look over perhaps

a thousand before I find it. Still, it is
true there are compensations. Valued old
friends, given up for years as lost or lent
(synonymous words when books are concerned), suddenly meet the eye. Senior's
Travel and Trout at the Antipodes, which
I had often looked for in vain, is in the
very spot where Henshall's *Book of the
Black Bass* used to be. At any rate I have,
as our American friends say, "located" one
book. Senior is where Henshall was. I
hope Henshall is not where Senior was—
behind and out of sight—or he won't reappear until the next earthquake.

I had, during many years, gradually
gathered together various editions of
Walton's *Angler*, of his Lives, works by
friends of Walton, or contemporary or
subsequent writers who refer to him.
These were of all sorts and sizes, but all
together ; now they are scattered to the
four corners of my library.

But if I have not found that reprint of
Walton with the error in it, I have found
a very pretty reprint by Mr. Elliot Stock,
published in 1877, also now out of print ;
but it has the correction.

In the first copies of the *Angler* struck
off for Richard Marriot there are some
verses near the end, which are thus referred
to by Walton.

Piscator, after listening to Viator's recitation of Sir Henry Wotton's verses in praise of angling, says :—

"Trust me, Scholer, I thank you heartily for these verses ; they be choicely good and doubtless made by a lover of angling. Come, now drink a glass to me and I will requite you with a very good copy of Verses ; it is a farewel to the vanities of the world, and some say written by Dr. D. ; but let them be writ by whom they will, he that writ them had a brave soul, and must needs be possest with happy thoughts at the time of their composure."

The last two lines of the verses run :—

" And if contentment be a stranger, then
I'l nere look for it, but in heaven again."

But in the first copies these lines were thus printed :—

" And if contention be a stranger, then
I'l nere look for it, but in heaven again."

As pointed out by Sir Harris Nicolas and by Mr. Westwood in his admirable *Chronicle of " The Compleat Angler,"* there are several other misprints in these first copies, such as " Fordig " for " Fordidg," " Padoch " for " Padock," etc. For a very minute account of the differences and additions in the five editions published during Walton's lifetime, I must refer the reader to Mr. Westwood's *Chronicle.**

Of all the scores of title-pages of editions of Walton's *Angler* none excels the first, reproduced on the opposite page.

THE DEDICATION.

In his dedication to the Right Worshipful John Offley, of Madely Manor, in the County of Stafford, Esq., Walton says :—

"MY MOST HONOURED FRIEND,—

"SIR,—I have made so ill use of your former faviors as by them to be encouraged to intreat that they may be enlarged to the patronage and protection of this Book ; and I have put on a modest confidence that I shall not be denied, because 'tis a discourse of Fish and Fishing, which you both know so well, and love and practice so much.

"You are assur'd (though there be ignorant men of another belief) that Angling is an Art ; and you know that Art better then any that I know : and that this is truth, is demōstrated by the fruits of that pleasant labor which you enjoy when you purpose to give rest to your mind, and devest your self of your more

* A small "remainder" of this work was purchased by Sampson Low, Marston, & Co., Ld.

The
Compleat Angler
or the
Contemplative man's
Recreation.

Being a Discourse of
FISH and FISHING,
Not unworthy the perusal of most *Anglers*.

Simon Peter *said. I go a fishing and they said. We
also wil go with thee. John* 21. 3.

London, Printed by *T. Maxey for Rich* MARRIOT, *in
S. Dunstans* Church-Yard. Fleet ſtreet. 1653.

serious business, and (which is often)
dedicate a day or two to this Recreation.

" At which time, if common Anglers
should attend you, and be eye-witnesses
of your success, not of your fortune, but
your skill, it would doubtless beget in
them an emulation to be like you, and
that emulation might beget an industrious
diligence to be so : but I know it is not
atainable by common capacities.

" Sir, this pleasant curiositie of Fish and
Fishing (of wch you are so great a Master)
has been thought worthy the pens and
practices of divers in other Nations, which
have been reputed men of great Learning
and Wisdome ; and amongst those of this
Nation, I remember Sir Henry Wotton (a
dear lover of this Art) has told me, that
his intentions were to write a discourse of
the Art, and in the praise of Angling, and
doubtless he had done so, if death had
not prevented him ; the remembrance of
which hath often made me sorry ; for, if
he had lived to do it, then the unlearned
Angler (of which I am one) had seen some
Treatise of this Art worthy his perusal,
which (though some have undertaken it)
I could never yet see in English.

" But mine may be thought as weak
and as unworthy of common view : and
I do here freely confess, that I should

rather excuse myself, then censure others, my own Discourse being liable to so many exceptions ; against which, you (Sir) might make this one, That it can contribute nothing to your knowledge ; and lest a longer Epistle may diminish your pleasure, I shall not adventure to make this Epistle longer then to add this following truth,

 " That I am really, Sir,
  " Your most affectionate Friend,
   " and most humble Servant
     " Iz. Wa."

In his " Epistles Dedicatory " and " Addresses to the Reader " Walton excels. There is such a pleasant, modest style and gentle humour about them, that the reader feels at once he is introduced to the company of no ordinary writer. It will be noticed that in the closing lines of the dedication just quoted there is an unnecessary repetition of the word " Epistle." On turning to his fifth edition—the last and most complete of those published in his lifetime—I find that he noticed this, altering the lines to—

" and lest a longer Epistle may diminish your pleasure, I shall make this no longer than to add," etc. He also altered "favor" to "favovr" "then" to "than" "demõstrated" to "demonstrated" etc.

9

THE ADDRESS TO THE READER.

This gives such a clear idea of the nature and object of his work that I shall quote it, giving the version finally revised by him, as it contains all that is in the first edition with some interesting additions.

"TO ALL READERS OF THIS DISCOURSE, BUT ESPECIALLY TO THE HONEST ANGLER.

"I think fit to tell thee these following truths, That I did neither undertake, nor write, nor publish, and much less own, this Discourse to please my self: and having been too easily drawn to do all to please others, as I propos'd not the gaining of credit by this undertaking, so I would not willingly lose any part of that to which I had a just title before I begun it, and therefore do desire and hope, if I deserve not commendations, yet, I may obtain pardon.

"And though this Discourse may be liable to some exceptions, yet I cannot but doubt but that most Readers may receive so much pleasure or profit by it, as may make it worthy the time of their perusal, if they be not too grave or too busie men. And this is all the confidence

that I can put on concerning the merit
of what is here offered to their consideration and censure ; and if the last prove
too severe, as I have a liberty, so I am
resolv'd to use it and neglect all sowre
Censures.

"And I wish the Reader also to take
notice, that in writing of it I have made
my self a recreation of a recreation ; and
that it might prove so to him, and not read
dull and tediously I have in several places
mixt (not any scurrility, but) some innocent harmless mirth ; of which, if thou be
a severe, sowre-complexioned man, then
I here disallow thee to be a competent
judge ; for Divines say, There are offences
given, and offences not given but taken.

"*And I am the willinger to justifie the
pleasant part of it, because though it is
known I can be serious at seasonable times,
yet the whole discourse is, or rather was,
a picture of my own disposition, especially
in such days and times as I have laid aside
business, and gone a fishing with honest
Nat. and R. Roe ; but they are gone, and
with them most of my pleasant hours, even
as a shadow, that passeth away, and
returns not.*

"And next let me add this, that he
that likes not the book, should like the
excellent picture of the Trout, and some

of the other fish; which I may take a
liberty to commend, because they concern
not myself.

"Next let me tell the Reader, that in
that which is the more useful part of this
Discourse, that is to say, the observations
of the nature and breeding, and seasons,
and catching of Fish, I am not so simple
as not to know, that a captious Reader
may find exceptions against something
said of some of these; and therefore I
must entreat him to consider, that experience teaches us to know, that several
Countries alter the time, and I think
almost the manner, of fishes breeding,
but doubtless of their being in season;
as may appear by three Rivers in Mon-
mouthshire, namely Severn, Wie, and
Usk, where Cambden (Brit. f. 633)*
observes, that in the River Wie, Salmon
are in season from Sept. to April, and we
are certain, that in Thames and Trent,
and in most other Rivers they be in
season the six hotter months.†

"Now for the Art of catching fish, that
is to say, how to make a man that was

* The editor of one edition of Walton turns
(Brit. f. 633) into (*British Fishes,* 633).

† If Walton had known the Wye as he did the
Thames and Trent, he would have corrected the
celebrated author of the *Britannia.*

none, to be an angler by a book? he that undertakes it shall undertake a harder task than Mr. Hales (a most valiant and excellent Fencer), who in a printed book (called, A private School of Defence) undertook to teach the art or science, and was laugh'd at for his labour. Not but that many useful things might be learnt by that book, but he was laugh'd at, because that art was not to be taught by words, but practice: and so must Angling. And note also, that in this Discourse I do not undertake to say all that is known, or may be said of it, but I undertake to acquaint the Reader with many things that are not usually known to every Angler; and I shall leave gleanings and observations enough to be made out of the experience of all that love and practice this recreation, to which I shall encourage them. For Angling may be said to be so much like the Mathematicks, that it can ne'er be fully learnt; at least not so fully, but that there will still be more new experiments left for the tryal of other men that succeed us.

"But I think that all that love this game may here learn something that may be worth their money, if they be not poor and needy men; and in case they be I then wish them to forbear to buy it: for

I write not to get money, but for pleasure, and this Discourse boasts of no more; for I hate to promise much and deceive the Reader.

"And however it proves to him, yet I am sure I have found a high content in the search and conference of what is here offer'd to the Reader's view and censure: I wish him as much in the perusal of it, and so I might here take my leave, but will stay a little and tell him, that whereas it is said by many, that in Flye-fishing for a Trout, the Angler must observe his 12 several flies for the twelve months of the year; I say, he that follows that rule, shall be as sure to catch fish, and, be as wise, as he that makes Hay by the fair days in an Almanack, and no surer; for those very flies that use to appear about and on the water in one month of the year, may the following year come almost a month sooner or later; as the same year proves colder or hotter; and yet in the following Discourse I have set down the twelve flies that are in reputation with many Anglers, and they may serve to give him some observations concerning them. And he may note that there are in Wales and other countries, peculiar flies, proper to the particular place or country; and doubtless unless a man makes a flie to counterfeit that very flie in that place, he is like to lose his labour or much of it: But for the generality, three or four flies neat and rightly made, and not too big, serve for a Trout in most Rivers all the Summer. And for Winter flie-fishing it is as useful as an Almanack out of date: And of these (because as no man is born an artist, so no man is born an Angler) I thought fit to give thee this notice.

"When I have told the Reader, that in this fifth Impression there are many enlargements, gathered both by my own observation, and the communication with friends, I shall stay him no longer than to wish him a rainy evening to read this following Discourse ; and that (if he be an honest Angler) the East wind may never blow when he goes a Fishing.

"I. W."

Let me refer the reader again to the lines which I have printed in italics in this copy of Walton's address to the reader. He tells us there that it is, "or rather was a picture of my own disposition." There is a touch of sadness in the "or rather was." Walton was over eighty when he wrote thus. His fishing companions, "honest Nat. and R. Roe," referred to in his first edition, are, he tells

us, dead. But if we had nothing but the
book itself to tell us what he was, we
should read his character aright. His
genial, broad-minded, generous, honest
spirit is stamped on every page. We shall
see presently in what estimation he was
held by some of the best men of his own
day and since. His book is aglow with
human interest, and in *this* lies its ever-
fresh, ever-enduring power to charm; he
clothed the dry bones of a practical
treatise on fishing with so attractive a
garb of joyous love of nature and human
nature, that he must indeed be a "severe
sowre-complexioned" man who cannot
love him.

In the "Amateur Angler's" copy of the
first edition is fastened a little manuscript
in faded ink, evidently written by some
admirer of Walton many years ago: the
only clue to the writer are the initials
W. E. I give some extracts from it :—

"In Longman's Catalogue for 1816.
"No. 5435, Walton's *Angler*, first edition,
London, 1653, £4 4s.
"No. 5436, Walton's *Angler*, enlarged by
Cotton, with Venables' *Experienc'd Angler*,
Russia, 1676, £3."

Then follows an account of the first five
editions taken from one of the editions
of Walton edited by Sir John Hawkins,

who, as I have at some length noticed in my edition of Walton, was indebted to Oldys for most of the information given in the Lives of both Walton and Cotton.

From this extract we find that the market value of a copy of the first edition of Walton was about £4 4s. in 1816. What is the value of it now? From a catalogue sent to me recently by Messrs. Pickering & Chatto, 66, Haymarket, London, containing an advertisement of a first edition of Walton, I quote the following :—

"We here offer a PERFECT COPY of this precious little gem, for every page is genuine, and there is not so much as a page in fac-simile. The last perfect copy brought by auction £310, and the present one we con-sider to be reasonably priced. The above is the first issue of first edition, and contains the misprint on page 245, 'contention' for 'contentment.'"

> "Fair first editions, duly prized,
> Above them all, methinks, I rate
> The tome where Walton's hand revised
> His wonderful receipts for bait."
> ANDREW LANG.

The price asked was £235. All good "Waltons" go to America. Messrs. Pickering & Chatto have since informed me they sold this fine copy to an American collector.

CHAPTER IX.

The Second Edition of *The Compleat Angler*—
The Illustrations—An Interesting Discovery
—The Third and Fourth Editions—The
more Important Fifth, with Cotton's Addition
—Venables' *Experienc'd Angler*, Published
with the Fifth Edition—Walton's Letter to
Venables, and some Account of the Latter—
Charles Cotton's "Instructions How to Angle
for a Trout or Grayling in a Clear Stream"—
Some Account of Cotton—His Friendship
with Walton — His Family Affairs and
Death.

THE SECOND EDITION OF "THE COM-
PLEAT ANGLER."

HIS was published by Richard
Marriot in 1655. I have only
seen one or two copies of it in
twenty-five years; and as Mr.
Westwood, quoting Mr. Bindley, the
eminent book-collector, points out, it is
even rarer than the first edition, although
it does not command the same high price.
By the way, what will a first edition be

worth, say, in 1993? Mr. Westwood, in 1883, puts the value of a fine perfect copy at "from £70 to £80, or even more." Now (1893), as we have just seen, the price asked is £235, and as much as £310 has been paid.

In the description of the second edition, Mr. Westwood, in his *Chronicle of "The Compleat Angler,"* says: "The success of Walton's first essay in angling literature seems to have stimulated him to increased effort in preparing the second for the press. The work was, in fact, all but re-written; more than one-third was added to its original bulk, and many improvements were introduced into it. The interlocutors are three in this edition : Piscator, Venator (who takes the place of Viator— we are sorry to lose Viator), and Auceps. The chapters are twenty-one in number, the type, however, being larger than in the previous edition."

Respecting the

ILLUSTRATIONS IN WALTON'S BOOK,

Mr. Westwood says: "The first edition contains engravings of the trout, pike, carp, tench, perch, and barbel (to the second are added plates of the bream, eel, loach, and bullhead). The engraver is

unknown ; but Pierre Lombart, a noted
Frenchman then resident in this country,
and engaged in illustrating books, and
also Faithorne and Vaughan, are possible
candidates for the honour. We know
that the last mentioned was employed by
Marriot on other work. These plates,
which are said, with little probability, to
have been of silver, served for the first
four editions, and were re-engraved in
reverse, by a less artistic hand, for the
fifth edition, a circumstance which has
escaped notice."

I see that Sir John Hawkins, in his
fourth edition of the *Angler*, has this note
about the illustrations :—

" Walton, in the year 1653, published,
in a very elegant manner, his *Compleat
Angler, or Contemplative Man's Recreation*, in small duodecimo, adorned with
exquisite cuts of most of the fish mentioned in it. The artist who engraved
them has been so modest as to conceal
his name ; but there is great reason to
suppose they are the work of Lombart,
who is mentioned in the *Sculptura* of
Mr. Evelyn ; and also that the plates were
of steel."

Mr. Westwood, usually so extremely
careful, had evidently overlooked this later
account of Walton's book by Hawkins,

or he would not have said that Hawkins
"fixes the date of the first edition at
about 1660." As noted above, Hawkins
gives the correct date, 1653.

What were the Illustrations in Walton copied from? An Interesting Discovery.

Until this evening, when writing these
lines, I had often wondered what the
artist who engraved the fish in Walton's
book copied them from. Had he the
fish themselves, or did he copy some exist-
ing illustrations? Knowing that Walton
frequently refers to the celebrated German
naturalist Gesner, I took down from the
shelf a copy of Dr. Conrad Forer's *Ausz-
furliche beschreibung und lebendige Conter-
factur aller und jeden Fischen, von dem
kleinsten Fischlein an bisz auff den grösten
Wallfisch,* being the second part of a magnificent folio volume of over one thousand
pages full of illustrations of animals,
birds, reptiles, fishes, etc. It is a revised
and enlarged German translation of
Doctor Conrad Gesner's work *Latein
erstmals beschrieben,* and was printed at
Frankfort by Johann Saur, and published
by Robert Cambier's Heirs in the year
1598. In this volume I found the

originals of the illustrations in Walton's
Angler. I do not say they were copied
from this particular edition of Gesner,
which, by the way, is not, as far as I can
trace, included in the *Bibliotheca Piscatoria*.
For beauty of typography and excellence
of illustration I know few works on fish
which can compare with this. The artist
must have had the living or dead subject
before him—except in the case of sea-
serpents, mermaids and men, devil-fish,
and other mythical beasts and fishes,
when he draws from the imaginations of
travellers splendidly.

Compare the illustrations of the loach
and bullhead in Walton, used also in
Venables' *Experienc'd Angler*, with those
in the 1598 edition of Forer's *Fishes*,
also the carp, bream, tench, and perch.
The trout and pike have not quite such
a strong resemblance, but of the rest I
think there can be no question. Walton
continually refers to Gesner's great work;
he evidently possessed a copy, and doubtless, when discussing the publication of
the first edition of his work with Richard
Marriot, they arranged to have reduced
copies of the Gesner illustrations engraved.
The illustrations added to the second
edition are evidently also taken from
Gesner.

The Eels and Great Frost of 1125.

By the way, I notice that Walton, in giving the story of the eels which died in the very cold winter of 1125, says that "they did by nature's instinct get out of the water into a stack of hay in a meadow upon drie ground, and there bedded themselves, but yet at last a frost kill'd them." I find that Dr. Forer's *Gesner* gives the reason of the eels leaving the water as "aus hassung der Kälte" ("from hatred of the cold "), and the cause of their death in the haystack as "wegen der Kälte und mangel desz Wassers" ("on account of the cold and want of water").

The Third and Fourth Editions of "The Compleat Angler."

"The third edition," says *The Chronicle of " The Compleat Angler,"* "was issued in 1661 ; but before many copies had been sold, and for some reason (not now discoverable, though possibly pecuniary), the sale of the book was transferred from Richard Marriot to Simon Gape ('near the Inner Temple Gate in Fleet Street'), by whom the remainder of the impression was sent forth, with a fresh title-page, dated 1664." A few minor additions and corrections were made in this edition, and the chapter on the Laws of Angling "appears for the first time."

The fourth edition was published in 1668, and "is a mere paginary reprint of the second, with the exception of the 'errata,' which are corrected in the work." This edition was "Printed for R. Marriot, and sold by Charles Harper, at his shop, the next door to the Crown near Sergeants-Inn in Chancery Lane."

The Fifth Edition of Walton and the First of Cotton.

The last edition of his work published during Walton's lifetime was the fifth, published in 1676. I have a copy of the fat little volume, 6 in. by 4, in its original binding, in which Walton's work is bound up with those of Venables and Cotton. In many respects this is the most interesting of all the editions. It was the last Walton had to do with, and the first which contained his friend Charles Cotton's " Instructions How to Angle for a Trout or Grayling in a Clear Stream," written with Walton's sanction as an addition to his work. It also contains a most characteristic letter from Walton to Venables, whom he thus addresses.

Walton's Letter to Colonel Venables.

To His Ingenious Friend the Author on his "Angling Improv'd."

" Honoured Sir,—Though I never (to my knowledg) had the happiness to see your Face, yet accidentally coming to a view of this Discourse before it went to the Press, I held myself obliged in point of gratitude for the great advantage I received thereby, to tender you my particular acknowledgment, especially having been for thirty years past, not only a Lover but a practiser of that innocent Recreation, wherein by your judicious Precepts I find my self fitted for a Higher Form ; which expression I take the boldness to use because I have read and practised by many Books of this kind, formerly made publick ; from which (although I received much advantage in the practick) yet (without prejudice to their worthy authors) I could never find in them that height of Judgment and Reason, which you have manifested in this (as I may call it) Epitome of Angling since my reading whereof, I cannot look upon some Notes of my own gathering, but methinks I do *puerilia tractare.* But

10

lest I should be thought to go about to magnifie my own Judgment, in giving yours so small a portion of its due, I humbly take leave with no more ambition than to kiss your hand, and to be accounted

Your humble and

thankful Servant,

"I. W."

COLONEL ROBERT VENABLES.

The first edition of *The Experienc'd Angler*, by Venables, was published by Richard Marriot in 1662. The best modern reprint is that published in 1827 by T. Gosden; it contains a memoir of the author, Colonel Robert Venables, from which it appears that he served in the Parliamentary army. In 1644 he was made Governor of Chester; in 1649 he was Commander-in-Chief of the Forces in Ulster. In 1654 Cromwell fitted out a fleet for the conquest of Hispaniola, and Colonel Venables and Admiral Penn were entrusted with the command. Gosden gives a long and interesting account of this unfortunate expedition, taken, he tells us, from a contemporary manuscript in his possession, which had not previously been printed

According to the writer, who was evidently no admirer of Cromwell, one of the objects of the expedition was to get Venables out of the way. " 'Twas doubtless," he says, "none of the least ends which that fox, Oliver, had in that design ; to rid himself of some persons whom he could neither securely employ, nor safely discard : which end seemed chiefly to influence the managery of the whole business, as you will perceive by the story."

During this expedition Venables appears to have acted with the greatest bravery and fortitude in the face of a series of most trying disasters. On one occasion, at the assault of a fort, " he being before brought very low with his flux, the toil of the day had so far spent him, that he could not stand or go but as supported by two ; and in that manner he moved from place to place, to encourage the men. But the latter he could not prevail on, neither by commands, entreaties, or offer of rewards. At last, fainting among them, he was carried off."

On their return to England in September, Venables and Penn were both imprisoned in the Tower. What became of Venables afterwards ? Gosden, writing in 1827, says : " His subsequent liberation, and the particulars of his life after this period, have baffled all attempts at discovery." It seems extraordinary that of a soldier so well known as Venables no trace can be found after his imprisonment in the Tower.

All we know about him after 1655 is that his book was published in 1662, and that Walton wrote the charming commendatory letter to him which I have already quoted. Although a great deal of his writing is evidently the result of actual experience as an angler, I think it is equally clear that he used the prose version of *The Secrets of Angling* as a basis for his work. Among the rivers and places he mentions as having experience of are " the Weever in Cheshire, the Sow in Staffordshire, the Blackwater in Ulster, Lough Neaugh, Tom Shanes Castle, Mountjoy, Antrim," etc. He has some brief but interesting references to salmon and salmon-fishing, and evidently, when stationed in different parts of England and Ireland, occupied his leisure time in angling. Want of space prevents a longer notice of the work of this brave soldier, devout man, and keen angler, whom Walton tells us he never had the happiness to meet face to face.

CHARLES COTTON AND HIS PART OF "THE COMPLEAT ANGLER."

It was not until the fifth edition of Walton's book appeared that his friend Cotton's " Instructions How to Angle for a Trout or Grayling in a Clear Stream " were added to it.

Charles Cotton, Oldys tells us, was descended of a worthy and honourable family, and was the grandson of Sir George Cotton, Knight, who died in 1613, leaving issue by Cassandra MacWilliam, his wife, two children, Charles and Cassandra. The latter died unmarried before 1649. Charles Cotton, the father of the author of the second part of *The Compleat Angler*, lived at one time at Ovingden, or Oving-dean, in the county of Sussex. He married Olive, the daughter of Sir John Stanhope, of Elvaston, in Derbyshire, by his first wife, Olive, daughter and heiress of Edward Beresford, of Beresford and Enson, in Staffordshire, and of Bentley, in the county of Derby. He succeeded to those estates in her right, and settled at Beresford. This lady, Olive Stanhope, died in 1614, aged about thirty-three years ; and Drayton, the poet, among his elegies, has one in her commendation. Her daughter, named likewise Olive, heiress to her mother, left, by her husband, Charles, before mentioned, one son, named also Charles Cotton, of Beresford, Esq., the subject of this notice.

Cotton's father's marriage connected him with the families of Stanhope, Cockayne Aston, Port, and others of the highest rank in the counties of Derby and Stafford. He was distinguished for his talents and accomplishments, and was the friend and companion of many of the most eminent of his contemporaries, including Fletcher, Herrick, Carew, Ben Jonson, Sir Henry Wotton, Dr. Donne, Selden, Lovelace, Davenant, May, Lord Chief Justice Vaughan, and the great Lord Clarendon, who describes him as having "all those qualities which in youth raise men to the reputation of being fine gentlemen ; such a pleasantness and gaiety of humour, such a sweetness and gentleness of nature, and such a civility and delightfulness in conversation, that no man, in the Court or out of it, appeared a more accomplished person ; all these extraordinary qualifications being supported by as extraordinary a clearness of courage and fearlessness of spirit, of which he gave too often manifestation."

Charles Cotton, son of the man thus described by Clarendon, was born on

April 28th, 1630. His father was at Cambridge University, and it is probable he was also ; but there is no direct evidence on this point.

" Besides his academic or classical learning, he was happy in a graceful address, and well versed in the modern languages. He was ardently attached to literature ; but, except a few poems, he wrote nothing which was published till after the Restoration. He probably went abroad when a young man, and he himself mentions his having been in France and other foreign countries. It is evident, says Oldys, that after he came to be settled at home, he was early in much esteem, and conversant with many persons of high rank and repute, more especially with his cousin, Sir Aston Cockayne, Bart., of Pooley, in Warwickshire, and Ashbourne, in the Peak, who was well known to the noted poets and wits of his time ; also with Thomas Flatman, Esq., barrister of the Inner Temple, Alexander Broome, Izaak Walton, and others."

I venture to think that the portrait of Charles Cotton which forms the frontispiece to vol. ii. of my " Lea and Dove " edition of *The Compleat Angler* is much the best which has been published. This photo-etching is from an exquisite painting

by Sir Peter Lely of Cotton when a
young man of twenty-seven; it bears the
date 1657.   Mrs. Evelyn Holden, of
Nuttall Temple, Nottingham, most kindly
gave me permission to have it photo-
graphed.

In 1658 Cotton's friend Lovelace, the
poet, died "in a mean lodging in Gun-
powder Alley, near Shoe Lane," and it is
pleasant to read Aubrey's statement that
"George Petty, haberdasher in Fleet
Street, carried twenty shillings to him
every Monday morning from Sir ———
Many and Charles Cotton, Esq., for
months, and was never repaid."

It is clear from his writings that Cotton,
like Walton, was a staunch Royalist.
Oldys says that, besides devoting himself
to literature, he employed himself also in
the   delightful   amusements   of   planting,
gardening, and, above all, the sober recreation of angling, in which he became
"by long practice and experience most
eminently expert."   It is to the fact that
he loved angling and was acquainted with
Izaak Walton that he owes most of his
posthumous fame.   One finds here and
there humour, power, and a graceful fancy
in his poems ; but these qualities were
possessed at least equally by many of his
contemporaries, whose very names are

almost forgotten, and whose writings are known only to the student.

Cotton appears to have asked Walton if he should supplement *The Compleat Angler* by some " particular directions " how to angle for a trout or grayling in a clear stream, to which Walton agreed. Nothing could be more modest than Cotton's letter accompanying his MS., or more kind and appreciative than Walton's reply ; and although Cotton's work lacks much of that peculiar charm which, as Doctor Zouch says, will always endear Walton's book even to those who care nothing about angling, it cannot be denied that it is a very worthy addition to, and completion of, *The Compleat Angler.* Cotton was an accomplished angler in the highest branches of the art ; his instructions are so clear and practical that it is quite certain he wrote from personal experience, and in this respect his work is more original than some of the practical parts of Walton's. Indeed, it may be said, that, while Walton is the father of general anglers, Cotton is the apostle of the trout and grayling fisherman, and many of his instructions have been but little improved upon, even to the present day. In one place he advises the use even in February, in case of a frost or snow, of "the smallest gnats, browns, and duns you can make."

That Cotton had but a poor opinion of London-made flies is clear from his reply to Viator, who had just told him that he likes a fly Cotton has made for him "admirably well, and it perfectly resembles a fly; but we about London, make the bodies of our flies both much bigger and longer, so long as almost to the very beard of the hook." "I know it very well," says Cotton, "and had one of those flies given me by an honest gentleman, who came with my father Walton to give me a visit; which, to tell you the truth, I hung in my parlour window to laugh at."

COTTON'S LETTER TO WALTON, SENT WITH HIS MS.

" *To my most Worthy Father and Friend,*
    "MR. IZAAK WALTON, THE ELDER.

"SIR,—*Being you were pleased some years past, to grant me your free leave to do what I have here attempted; and observing, you never retract any promise when made in favour even of your meanest friends; I accordingly expect to see these following particular Directions for the taking of a Trout, to wait upon your better and more*

*general Rules for all sorts of Angling:
And though mine be neither so perfect, so
well digested, nor indeed so handsomely
coucht as they might have been, in so long
a time as since your leave was granted;
yet I dare affirm them to be generally true:
And they had appeared too in something a
neater dress, but that I was surpriz'd with
the suddain news of a suddain new edition
of your Compleat Angler; so that, having
but a little more than ten days time to turne
me in, and rub up my memory (for in truth
I have not in all this long time, though I
have often thought on't, and almost as often
resolv'd to go presently about it), I was
forc't upon the instant to scribble what I
here present you: which I have also endeavour'd to accommodate to your own Method.
And, if mine be clear enough for the honest
Brothers of the Angle readily to understand; (which is the only thing I aim at)
then I have my end; and I shall need to
make no further Apology; a writing of this
kind not requiring (if I were Master of any
such thing) any Eloquence to set it off, or
recommend it; so that if you, in your better
Judgment, or Kindness rather, can allow
it passable for a thing of this nature; You
will then do me honour if the Cypher fixt
and carv'd in the front of my little fishing-
house may be here explained: And, permit*

*me to attend you in publick, who in private
have ever been, am, and ever resolve to be,*
              " *Sir,*
     " *Your most affectionate*
        " *Son and Servant,*
             " CHARLES COTTON.
"BERISFORD, 10*th of March*, 167$\frac{2}{3}$."

To this letter Walton replied as follows :—

     " *To my most Honoured Friend*
     "CHARLES COTTON, ESQ.

" SIR,—You now see, I have return'd you,
your very pleasant, and useful discourse
of the Art of *Flie-Fishing* Printed, just as
'twas sent me : for I have been so obedient
to your desires, as to endure all the
praises you have ventur'd to fix upon me
in it. And when I have thankt you for
them, as the effects of an undissembled
love : then, let me tell you, Sir, that I will
endeavour to live up to the character you
have given of me, if there were no other
reason ; yet for this alone, that you, that
love me so well, may not, for my sake,
suffer by a mistake in your Judgment.

And, Sir, I have ventur'd to fill a part
of your Margin, by way of Paraphrase, for
the Readers clearer understanding the
situation both of your *Fishing-House*, and
the pleasantness that you dwell in. And

I have ventur'd also to give him a Copy
of Verses, that you were pleas'd to send
me, now some Years past; in which he
may see a good Picture of both; and, so
much of your own mind to, as will make
any Reader that is blest with a Generous
Soul, to love you the better. I confess, that
for doing this you may justly Judg me too
bold: if you do, I will say so too: and so
far commute my offence, that, though I
be more than a hundred Miles from you,
and in the eighty third year of my Age,
yet I will forget both, and next month
begin a Pilgrimage to beg your pardon,
for, I would dye in your favour: and till
then will live,

   " Sir,
  " Your most affectionate
   " Father and Friend,
    " Izaak Walton.

 "London, *April* 29*th*, 1676."

It will be noticed that Cotton, in his
letter to Walton, says he has endeavoured
to accommodate the method of his work
to Walton's—that is to say, has put it into
the form of "A Discourse" between
"Piscator Junior" (himself) and "Viator."
I think he succeeded admirably, his
imaginary conversations being almost as
natural, and quite as instructive as those

between the characters in Walton, while he never loses an opportunity of speaking in warmest praise of his old friend. I must give a quotation or two from him, as showing the esteem and affection in which Walton was held by the handsome soldier-courtier, and man of the world, Charles Cotton.

James Russell Lowell wrote an " Introduction" to an edition of *The Complete Angler* published in 1889 by Messrs. Little, Brown, & Company, of Boston, U.S.A., and it is pleasant to find such a writer has no stone to throw at Cotton; for, indeed, editor after editor has almost erected a monument to him in this fashion. It is true that he, like Donne, wrote some verse, of which he, like Donne, was doubtless afterwards ashamed. As Lowell says : "Cotton was a man of genius, whose life was cleanlier than his muse always cared to be. If he wrote the *Virgil Travesty*, he also wrote verses which the difficult Wordsworth could praise, and a poem of gravely noble mood addressed to Walton on his Lives, in which he shows a knowledge of what goodness is that no bad man could have acquired. Let one line of it at least shine in my page, not as a sample, but for its own dear sake :—

'For in a virtuous act all good men share.' "

I hope to refer again to Lowell's "Introduction" when noticing some of the later editions of the *Angler*.

After this kindly reference to him, I will give one or two quotations from his work, which surely were written with sincerity, and, being so, are themselves witnesses for the good in Cotton's character.

COTTON'S OPINION OF WALTON.

" *Viator.* You go far, Sir, in the praise of your Country Rivers, and I perceive have read Mr. Walton's *Compleat Angler* by your naming of *Hantshire*, and I pray what is your opinion of that Book?

" *Piscator Junr.* My opinion of Mr Walton's Book is the same with every man's, that understands anything of the Art of Angling, that it is an excellent good one, and that the fore mentioned Gentleman understands as much of Fish, and Fishing, as any Man living : but I must tell you further, that I have the happiness to know his person, and to be intimately acquainted with him, and in him to know the worthiest Man, and to enjoy the best and the truest Friend any Man ever had : nay, I shall yet acquaint you further, that he gives me leave to call him Father, and I hope is not yet asham'd to own me for his adopted Son. . . . My father Walton will be seen twice in no Man's company he does not like, and likes none but such as he believes to be very honest men, which is one of the best Arguments, or at least of the best Testimonies I have, that I either am, or that he thinks me one of those, seeing I have not yet found him weary of me.

" *Viator.*   You speak like a true Friend, and in doing so render your self worthy of his friendship."

That the friendship between Walton and Cotton, which found so charming an expression in their letters and works, was continued to the last, is proved by the fact that, in Walton's will, dated August 16th, 1683, among those named to receive a ring, with the motto "A friend's farewell, I. W., obiit," was "Mr. Chas. Cotton,"— a fitting end to one of the most delightful episodes in literary history.

COTTON'S FAMILY AFFAIRS AND DEATH.

Cotton was married about the year 1656 to Isabella, daughter of Sir Thomas Hutchinson, of Owthorp, by whom he had three sons and five daughters. He was married a second time, his second wife being the widow of Wingfield Cromwell,

Earl of Ardglass, by whom he had no children, and who survived him.

For many years before his death Cotton was often in great pecuniary difficulties. In answer to a letter of mine asking if possibly some unpublished papers relative to Charles Cotton existed, Mr. Philip Beresford Hope, the present owner of Beresford Dale, very kindly replied as follows :—

" Dear Sir,—Many thanks for your letter. I am afraid we have no unpublished papers relative to Charles Cotton. If it would be of any use to you, I could let you have some photographs and drawings of Beresford Hall in a partially ruined state, before it was pulled down. I do not know whether you are aware of a cave in the limestone rocks in Beresford Dale, well hidden from view, in which Charles Cotton is *popularly* reported to have hidden from his creditors for some weeks, and to have evaded them. I am also unaware if you are cognisant of the fact that the interior of Cotton's Fishing-House was at one time frescoed with paintings of piscatorial and other sporting subjects. I will, on my return to town, make a search for any unpublished matter relative to Charles Cotton, and if I come across any, I will communicate with you. I must thank you very much for the beautiful plate of Pike Pool you sent me.

"Yours truly,

(Signed) " P. BERESFORD HOPE."

The plate Mr. Beresford Hope refers to is one of Pike Pool, by Mr. Geo. Bankart, which appears in the "Lea and Dove" edition of the *Angler*.

Cotton is supposed to have died of a fever on February 13th, 1687, only four years after the death of his old friend Walton. By an act of administration of his effects upon his decease, dated September 12th, 1687, it appears his principal creditrix was Elizabeth Bludworth, and he is described as of the parish of St. James, Westminster. His son, Beresford Cotton, commanded a company in a regiment of foot raised by the Earl of Derby for the service of King William; one of his daughters married Dr. Geo. Stanhope, Dean of Canterbury.

CHAPTER X.

An Estimate of the Influence of Walton's Book
on Angling and Angling Literature—It can
Never be Antiquated—Has Kept the True
Sporting Instinct Alive—Diversity of Baits
Recommended by Walton—His Chapter on
Trout-Fishing—The Celebrated Fordidge
Trout—Walton and his Editors—What
would He think of Some of our Modern Auto-
matic Angling Appliances?—His Religion
—His Reference to Hampshire Streams—
Notes on other Chapters of His Book—A Tip
for Dry-Fly Anglers—Did Walton Keep a
Horse?—His Directions for Bream, Barbel,
and other Fishing—Fishing-Tackle Makers
Mentioned by Walton—His Chapter on Fish-
Ponds—A Drink like Nectar.

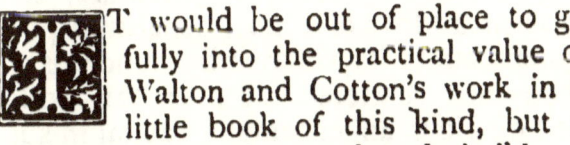

"THE COMPLEAT ANGLER" FROM AN
ANGLER'S POINT OF VIEW.

IT would be out of place to go
fully into the practical value of
Walton and Cotton's work in a
little book of this kind, but a
few general remarks may be admissible.

Compared with all that had preceded
it, it can certainly be said not only to

163

justify its title, but to have at once become the standard text-book of angling. That the anglers of Walton's day fully appreciated it is proved by the five editions published before he died ; and since then the demand for it, especially during the last century, has been such that more than one hundred editions have been called for,— not, of course, that all these editions have been produced to meet the wants of those who wish to learn the art of angling : its other, higher, and far more lasting merits are becoming more and more responsible for the continued demand for it. Since angling books have been produced in such numbers that the literature of the subject is more voluminous than that of almost any other, since the art has been so elaborated that volumes are devoted to one fish and the methods of its capture, it can no longer be said that *The Compleat Angler* is complete. But it is mainly responsible for this vast literature, this widespread love of a most delightful sport, which counts its votaries by hundreds of thousands scattered all over the world, and employs an enormous capital in supplying their wants.

But in spite of all our modern knowledge, I should still recommend those who would learn what angling is to go to the pages of the "tenderest teacher and powerfullest preacher" our art has ever had. What may be missing in science can be found elsewhere, and will be more than made up for by his description of what we may call the essence of the art, by the simple, often quaint, but always perfect expositions of the true spirit of angling which are given in his book as in none other.

I confess I cannot understand those anglers—and I have met some—who scoff at Walton as being antiquated. In mere practical details he may not always be equal to that scientific, mechanical precision in angling for which we have, in my humble opinion, far too much admiration in the present day ; but as a teacher of all that part of angling which is most worthy our enthusiasm and love, Walton is not and never can be antiquated.

For instance, I open his book at random, and find a strong argument in favour of the keeping of fence months : —

" The not keeping of Fence months for the preservation of Fish will in time prove the destruction of all rivers. . . . He that shall view the wise statutes made in the 13 of Edw. the I. and the like in Rich. the III. may see several provisions made against the destruction of Fish : and though I profess no knowledge of the Law, yet I am sure the regulation of these defects might be easily mended. But I remember that a wise friend of mine did usually say, *That which is every bodies business, is no bodies business.* If it were otherwise, there could not be so many Nets and Fish that are under the statute size, sold daily amongst us, and of which the *Conservators* of the Waters should be ashamed.

"But above all, the taking Fish in spawning time, may be said to be against nature ; it is like taking the dam from her nest when she hatches her young."

It is a bold thing to say, but I doubt if these words of Walton had not been ringing down the centuries ever louder and louder, that our fresh-water fisheries would have long ago been destroyed. These and many similar passages in which unfair and unseasonable fishing is denounced have kept alive the true sporting instinct among anglers, and enabled them of late years, when by combination they became powerful, to obtain from our governments laws for the protection of their interests which as individuals they asked for in vain.

As regards many of the baits recommended by Walton, present-day anglers have, as a rule, no knowledge of them, and much of the want of sport complained of, in such well-stocked and well-protected rivers as the Lea, Thames, and Trent, is due to the continual use of the same baits and ground-baits, and the overdosing the fish with the latter. The British angler treats the fish pretty much as his wife treats him: it is beef and mutton one week, and mutton and beef the next. Walton taught the use of a great variety of baits; and when worms, paste, and gentles failed, knew a dozen as good to try. Most of the wild fruits and berries are food for birds when ripe, and some kinds of fish take them also. I remember once, when fishing for large bream in a deep pool, being unable to obtain even a nibble with the three stock baits of to-day—gentles, worms, and paste; but noticing some ripe blackberries overhanging the water, I determined to try them as bait, and very soon had two or three good fish, and often afterwards made good use of that and similar pleasant baits to which the fish had become accustomed, after a little trouble on my part in baiting a place or two. I think the sense of smell is very strong in some fish. Tench, for instance, I often found would take a paste made of brown bread when one of white was not touched.

Chub-fishing is Piscator's first lesson to Venator in practical angling. It is evidently a bit of personal experience, probably near Amwell Magna, on the Lea, a portion of that fishful stream in which chub still abound. The description is perfect, a word-picture of what every chub-fisher has often experienced when fishing in a stream where these handsome fish abound. The natural grasshopper, a bait often recommended by Walton, is often far more killing than a worm, and yet one nowadays rarely finds it used.

My father, the " Amateur Angler," first taught me to catch a trout or a chub by dapping with a blue-bottle fly, holding the rod over an alder bush or casting an artificial fly in a stream, and in return I, over five-and-twenty years after, showed him how to float a dry fly over a rising trout or grayling in Hampshire and Derbyshire. What delightful days I have had with him on our English streams, days the remembrance of which makes me hope the future may have many such in store!

Of the nature of the chub, and the best baits to use at different seasons for him, Walton has left but little for later writers to add; and if this fish can be made into a decent dish of food, it must surely be by following his directions.

" Observations of the nature and breeding of the Trout, and how to fish for him
—and the Milk Maid's Song," is the heading of the much enlarged Chapter IV.
of the fifth edition; perhaps the most
interesting of all Walton wrote. He loved
the trout above all fish, and held trout-
fishing in the greatest estimation. Among
the varieties of this fish which he mentions none has caused more controversy
than the famous " Fordidge Trout ": his
statements have been flatly contradicted
by some of his editors. He says,—

" There is also in *Kent* near *Canterbury*
a Trout (call'd there a Fordidge Trout),
a *Trout* (that bears the name of the Town
where it is usually caught) that is accounted
the rarest of Fish ; many of them near the
bigness of a *salmon*, but known by their
different colour, and in their best season
they cut very white; and none of these
have been known to be caught with an
Angle, unless it were one that was caught
by Sir George Hastings ; and he hath told
me, he thought that *Trout* bit not for
hunger but wantonness, and it is the
rather to be believed, because both he
then, and many others before him, have
been curious to search into their bellies,
what the food was by which they lived ;
and have found out nothing by which

they might satisfy their curiosity." . . .
Walton then states that this fish "knows
his times (I think almost his day) of coming into that river out of the sea, where
he lives (and it is like, feeds) nine months
out of the year, and fasts three in the
River of Fordidge. . . . You are to know
that this Trout is thought to eat nothing
in the fresh water."

So far Walton; now, in his excellent
edition of *The Compleat Angler*, Dr.
Bethune has this reference to Walton's
Fordidge Trout :—

"Fordwich is about two miles east of
Canterbury, on the river the Stour.
Yarrell says, unhesitatingly, that the Fordwich trout is the *salmon trout* (*Salmo trutta*
of Linnæus, *Salmo albus* or white trout,
Flem, *Brit. An.*), what is called the *hirling*
in some parts of Scotland. He says also,
in contradiction to Walton and his friend
Sir George Hastings, that quantities are
taken with the rod, and on being examined
are found full of various insects, particularly the sand-hopper. The very rapid
digestion of the salmon family led to our
author's error."

This is a fair specimen of the manner
in which Walton is flatly contradicted, and
yet I feel certain that he is perfectly right
and Yarrell wrong. I was for some years

a member of the Stour Fishery Association,
and have caught trout both above and
below Canterbury. I have not been able
to see a specimen of the fish Walton
refers to ; but experienced salmon anglers
living at Canterbury have, and they agree
with me in thinking that the fish is the
Bull Trout (*salmo eriox*) which ascends
several of our south-coast rivers. This fish
corresponds with Walton's description,
and only very rarely in this river is one
taken on a rod and line, and nothing is
ever found in its stomach. If I am not
mistaken, my late friend Frank Buckland
was the first to identify Walton's Fordidge
Trout with the Bull Trout, and his opinion
on a point of that kind was second to
none.

And yet another editor of Walton,
" Ephemera " (Fitzgibbon), says the whole
of Walton's account of the Fordidge Trout
is a mere fable.

In fact, these editors of Walton who,
generation after generation, impose upon
themselves the task of correcting in foot-
notes his mistakes, or supposed mistakes,
seem to me to spend much labour in vain ;
for, as one of them remarks, " Very mucn
of what Walton says the reader will at
once see to be erroneous." Then why go
to the trouble of correcting him, especially

when the "corrections" are often more erroneous than the original?

To writers like "Ephemera" is due the vague impression which some anglers have who have not read Walton, that he was merely a bottom or live-bait fisher, and knew next to nothing of fly-fishing or spinning with a minnow. This statement is far from being correct. Again, both Walton and Cotton have suffered by the want of angling knowledge of their illustrators. Who does not remember the picture entitled "Landing the Grayling," which has appeared in so many editions of Walton, in which the angler is represented as catching hold of the line to pull the fish in? And yet over a century before this engraving was made Walton wrote thus:—

"*Piscator.* Look you scholar, you see I have hold of a good Fish: I now see it is a Trout, I pray, put that net under him, and *touch not my line, for if you do, then we break all.* Well done scholar, I thank you."

And Cotton, in the very incident depicted, makes Piscator Junior call out "Bring hither that landing net, Boy."

It is true, as I have previously mentioned, that Walton quotes Barker's directions for fly-fishing and fly-making "with-

out much variation," as he tells us in his
first edition ; but it does not follow that he
knew nothing about it himself. Cotton
distinctly tells us " it would look like a pre-
sumption in me, and peradventure would
do so in another man, to pretend to give
lessons for angling after him [Walton],
who I do really believe understands as
much of it, at least as any man in England "; and he explains that it is the style
of fishing necessitated by the very clear
waters he fished in that he will describe.
In another place he tells Viator he will
give him some instructions how " to angle
for a Trout in a clear River, that my Father
Walton himself will not disapprove, though
he did either purposely omit, or did not
remember them, when you, and he sate
discoursing under the *Sycamore* Tree."

"Ephemera" says how astonished
Walton would have been could he have
seen the artificial minnows and other baits
made nowadays. Yes, he would indeed
have been astonished ; but if he wished to
kill a dish of trout, I think he would still
prefer that beautiful artificial minnow he so
lovingly describes, "made by a handsome
Woman that had a fine hand, and a live
Minnow lying by her" to copy. His description of the way to make a natural
or artificial minnow spin so that "a large

trout will come as fiercely at it as the highest mettled Hawk doth seize on a Partridge, or a Grey-hound on a Hare," wants no improving.

It would, I think, be a good thing if in many ways we went back to the simplicity of Walton's directions in making up our tackles—spinning or other. I can fancy his astonishment if a modern "compleat angler" could show him the latest kill-devil with great metal fans to spin it, and carrying from six to fifteen hooks; what would he as a sportsman say to the "automatic" and other inventions for taking fish which are so loudly advertised in this country and America, their chief merits—if their inventors are right—being that they give the fish "no chance"? Some are guaranteed to kill the fish by spring power, so that he cannot breathe, two springs made into hooks holding his jaws open.

With such tackle and baits Walton would never have killed that three brace of trout before breakfast; but, on the other hand, he would never have had to make Piscator exclaim,—

"Oh me! he has broke all; there's half a line and a good hook lost.

" *Venator.* Aye and a good trout too.

" *Piscator.* Nay, the Trout is not lost,

for take notice no man can lose what he
never had."

Then follow fly-fishing and fly-making;
and it surely does not follow that, because
Walton tells us he gives the directions of
Barker and another first-rate fly-fisher, he
knew nothing about it himself. It is clear
to me that he was a good all-round angler,
and was experienced in all the styles of
fishing he describes.

The rest of this chapter is a most pleasant mixture of fishing and other lore and
praise of nature and thanks to God; one
very marked characteristic of Walton
being that his religion is so purely and
genuinely a part of himself that, though
he brings it in at all sorts of odd seasons,
it is never out of place and never offends.
As Lowell says, " The reader of the
Angler finds himself conscious of one
meaning in the sixth Beatitude too often
overlooked,—that the pure in heart shall
see God, not only in some future and
far-off sense, but wherever they turn their
eyes."

" *Piscator.* And now, Scholar, my
direction for the flie-fishing is ended with
this showre, for it has done raining; and
now look about you, and see how plea-
santly that Meadow looks; nay, and the
Earth smells as sweetly too. Come, let

me tell you that holy Mr. Herbert says
of such days and flowers as these, and
then we will thank God that we enjoy
them, and walk to the River and sit down
quietly, and try to catch the other brace
of trouts." And then he quotes Herbert's
verses,—

> " Sweet day, so cool, so calm, so bright,
> The bridal of the earth and skie,
> Sweet dews shall weep thy fall to-night,
> For thou must die."

Walton, in his Life of Herbert, tells us
he had seen him, though he was not personally acquainted with him, and makes
Venator say he " had heard he loved
angling."

It was while sitting under the sycamore,
as, he reminds us, " Virgil's Tityrus and
his Melibæus did under their broad beech-
tree," that Walton says,—

"No life my honest Scholar, no life so
happy and so pleasant, as the life of a
well governed *Angler* ; for when the
Lawyer is swallowed up with business,
and the Statesman is preventing or con-
triving plots, then we sit on Cowslip-
banks, hear the birds sing, and possess
ourselves in as much quietness as these
silent silver streams, which we now see
glide so quietly by us. Indeed my Good
Scholar, we may say of Angling, as Dr.

Boteler said of Strawberries, Doubtless God could have made a better berry, but doubtless God never did : And so (if I might be Judge) *God never did make a more calm, quiet, innocent recreation than Angling.*"

Some few years ago, when we were wondering what few words we could put under the memorial of the late Francis Francis * in Winchester Cathedral, I suggested to Mr. Senior those italicised above, and these words from Walton are now engraved there.

Walton frequently refers to the trout and trout rivers of Hampshire. In one place he says :—

" *Piscator.* And you are to know that in Hampshire, which I think exceeds all England for swift, shallow, clear, pleasant Brooks, and store of Trouts, they use to catch Trouts in the night, by the light of a Torch or Straw, which when they have discovered, they strike with a *Trout spear* or other wayes. This kind of way they catch very many, but I would not believe it till I was an eye-witness of it, nor do I like it now I have seen it.

" *Venator.* But Master, do not Trouts see us in the night?

* For many years angling editor of *The Field,* author of *A Book of Angling,* etc.

"*Piscator.* Yes, and hear, and smell too, both then and in the daytime."

I have heard anglers doubt if fish have much if any sense of smell; but Walton was undoubtedly right, as any angler who is not careful to use fresh and sweet baits and ground-baits will discover. Chapter VI., a short one, is entitled "Observations of the Umber or Grayling and directions how to fish for them." It shows Walton was well acquainted with the habits of this fish, which is, he says, "very pleasant and jolly after mid-April," but "not to me so good to eat or to angle for" as the trout. Walton mentions that "he has been taken with a fly made of the red feathers of a Parakita"; in our day the "Red Tag" has slain its thousands of grayling, so it would seem a red colour has some special attraction for this fish, which is scented as of water-thyme, and the pupils of whose eyes are pear-shaped.

By the way, Walton's mention of Hampshire brooks reminds me that in the verses entitled "The Angler's Wish," which he tells Venator he made "when I sate last on this Primrose-bank," occur the lines,—

"Or, with my Bryan, and a book,
   Loyter long days near Shawford-brook."

These verses appeared first in the third edition of the *Angler*, published in 1661. It has generally been assumed, and I have no doubt correctly so, that Shawford is short for Shallowford, the village on the Sow, near Stafford, where Walton owned a house and land which he left to the poor of Stafford. But we know that Walton was acquainted with Hampshire. I have just quoted a passage in which he tells us he had witnessed trout-spearing there by torchlight. This passage appears in the first edition, published in 1653. Is it not just possible that the Shawford referred to is the village of that name near Twyford, on the Itchen, a little below Winchester? I confess the probability is that Shallowford, near Stafford, is referred to, as he bought the farm in 1654,* and probably often visited it between that date and the time he wrote the verses referred to first published in 1661. However, I never pass Shawford, when fishing in the Itchen, without thinking of Walton.

Although he does not tell us so in so many words, we may gather from the text that the primrose bank on which the verses were composed was neither at Shawford nor Shallowford, but on the Lea

* By an error I have this as 1656 in the "Lea and Dove" edition of the *Angler.*—R. B. M.

not far from Waltham Cross ; for he says :
"When I had ended this composure, I
left this place and saw a Brother of the
Angle sit under that *hony-suckle hedg* (one
that will prove worth your acquaintance).
I sate down by him, and presently we met
with an accidental piece of merriment,
which I will relate to you ; for it rains
still." Then follows the amusing interlude
of the discussions and disputes between
the gang of gipsies and the gang of
beggars, the latter deciding at last to refer
their squabble for settlement " to old
Father Clause whom *Ben Johnson** in his
Beggars-bush created King of the Corporation," who "was that night to lodg
at an Ale-house (called *Catch-her-by-the-
way*) not far from Waltham Cross, and in
the high-road towards London."

Although the reel is mentioned by
Walton as used in salmon and pike-fishing
(I have already referred to what Barker
says about it), it is pretty clear that he did
not use it when trout-fishing, or fishing
in such a river as the Lea or Dove, or
he would not have replied as he did to
Venator, who exclaims,—

"Oh me, look you Master, a fish a fish,
oh las Master, I have lost her !

"*Piscator.* I marry Sir, that was a good

* Fletcher, not Jonson.

fish indeed; if I had had the luck to
have taken up that Rod, then 'tis twenty
to one, he should not have broke my line
by running to the rods end as you suffered
him : I would have held him within the
bent of my Rod (unless he had been fellow
to the great *Trout* that is near an ell long,
which was of such length and depth, that
he had his picture drawn, and now is to
be seen at mine Host Rickabies at the
George in Ware), and it may be, by giving
that very great trout the Rod, that is, by
casting it to him into the water, I might
have caught him at the long run, for so
I use alwayes to do when I meet with an
overgrown fish, and you will learn to do
so too hereafter; for I tell you, Scholar,
fishing is an Art, or at least, it is an Art
to catch fish."

In the absence of any reserve of line
on a reel, and with a rod which would
float, Walton's advice is sound enough.
Some correspondent of *The Fishing Gazette*,
who had campaigned in Afghanistan, described how the native fishermen captured
the heaviest fish in this way. Dr. Bethune
says, "This bungling practice is condemned
by Cotton, and should never be resorted
to by any one who has a reel at his hand."
Cotton had no chance of meeting with
a great Lea trout, and Walton had no

reel; it would have been more "bungling," in my opinion, to let the fish break the line than to risk rod and line, as he did in order to have a good chance of killing it.

Chapter VII. treats of "The Salmon, with directions how to fish for him."

Although erroneous in some particulars, Walton's general description of the habits of the salmon is very good. If his knowledge of actual fishing for this fish was confined to the Trent and Thames, his observation that baits are better than flies still holds—at least of the Trent, for the Thames has long ceased to produce salmon. Fly-fishing for Trent salmon has often been tried, but almost, if not quite, unsuccessfully. Here is Walton's reference to the use of the reel. "Note also, that many use to fish for a Salmon with a ring of wire on the top of their Rod, through which the Line may run to as great a length as is needful when he is hook'd. And to that end, some use a wheel about the middle of their Rod, or near their hand, which is to be observed better by seeing one of them, than by a large demonstration of words."

Chapter VIII. contains "Observations of the Luce or Pike, with directions how to fish for him."

For no statement has Walton been more

ridiculed than for saying that some pike
are bred of a weed called Pickerel-weed,
and yet the statement is not his; he merely
says it is so " unless learned Gesner be
much mistaken." His description of the
nature and habits of this fish is excellent,
and his stories about it, both native and
foreign, most interesting, and quite equal
to the best of our modern fish tales. His
directions for killing pike with a live bait
might be followed with advantage by
keepers on trout preserves where pike
have to be kept down. As Dr. Bethune
says, " Walton understood the pike well."

Chapter IX. deals with the carp and
" how to fish for him." Here, again, one of
Walton's fish stories—*i.e.*, that of the carp
being killed by the frogs—has proved to be
a true bill, full details of such killing being
given a few years ago in the columns of
Die Deutsche Fischerei Zeitung. Walton
rightly calls the carp "a stately, a good,
and a very subtil fish." In some rivers
and in some ponds I have experienced
the truth of his statement that the carp
is " very hard to take "; in others he bites
freely enough at any of the many excellent
baits given by Walton, who, among other
" tips," mentions the advantage of putting
a bit of scarlet cloth soaked in Oyl of
Peter, called by some Oyl of the Rock, on

the hook with the bait. If he did not invent it (and no one dare claim to invent anything nowadays), at any rate, dry fly-fishers have to thank Mr. Thomas Andrews, the celebrated pisciculturist of Guildford, for publishing the plan of oiling your fly with petroleum, or Oyl of Peter as Walton calls it. I have constantly proved its efficacy in keeping the fly dry, and am inclined to agree with Walton that fish rather like the smell of this oil. Mr. Andrews' plan—and I have found it answer admirably—is to carry a little oil in one of those small thick glass ink-bottles with inverted neck which prevents spilling. Have a small camel's-hair brush fixed into the bottom of the cork, so that when you remove the latter you have oil on the brush ready for use. The bottle can be suspended inside your creel, or from a button of your fishing-coat. N.B.—The fly floats better *after* the first few casts, and well-hackled flies answer best, of course. It is a tip which has done much to put the duffer at dry fly-fishing on a level with the expert on *the* point of all— viz., keeping your fly floating *on*, and not half-drowned *in*, the water. There is one of Walton's recipes for making a carp bait which some nights recently I heartily wished might become popular—viz., "Take the flesh of a cat cut small and bean flour, and beat them together in mortar with sugar or honey, etc."

Observations of the Bream, and directions to catch him" occupy Chapter X.

Of the truth of most of Walton's observations about carp, bream, tench, etc., I have had personal experience, having for many years possessed a deep pool of from two to three acres well stored with these fish. Walton says that "Bream breed exceedingly in a water that pleases him ; yea, in many Ponds so fast, as to over-store them, and starve the other fish." This I found to be the case with my bream.

Walton lived in the centre of London, and had some distance to go before he could fish in the Lea near Waltham, or Hoddesdon, or Ware. He could not go by train or tram or 'bus, as the modern Londoner does. He could not walk ; at least, if he did, he got little time for fishing. He could do it comfortably if he kept a horse ; and from a word or two let drop by accident in this chapter on bream-fishing I conclude he did keep a horse. In the midst of some directions for bream and carp baits and fishing, which have never been improved upon, among other things he tells Venator to "take a peck, or a peck and a half of sweet gross-ground barly-malt, and boil it in a kettle (one or two warms is enough) ; then strain it through a Bag into a tub (*the liquor whereof hath often done my Horse much good*), and when the bag and malt is near cold, take it down to the water-side about eight or nine of the clock in the evening, and not before ; cast in two parts of your ground bait, squeezed hard between both your hands ; it will sink presently to the bottom, and be sure it may rest in the very place where you mean to angle ; if the stream run hard or move a little, cast your Malt in handfuls a little the higher, upwards the stream. You may between your hands close the Malt so fast in handfuls, that the water will hardly part it with the fall.

"Your ground thus baited, and tackling fitted, leave your bag with the rest of your tackling and ground bait near the sporting-place all night, and in the morning about three or four of the clock visit the water-side (but not too near), for they have a cunning Watch-man and are watchful themselves too."

I have quoted more than I intended to, but the whole paragraph is very interesting to any one who cares about bream, carp, or tench-fishing, and it brings in Walton's horse. I have no doubt now that he used to ride out to his fishing and put up his horse at Host Rickabie's at the George in Ware, or at some other of those convenient inns near the river of which he has given such pleasant pictures.

In this chapter he tells us that he has often taken a pike a yard long on his bream hooks, but sometimes "he [the pike] hath had the luck to share my line." So he advises trying with a live bait at a baited spot like this, to get rid of any pike or perch which may be in the swim.

Dr. Bethune, most careful of annotators, evidently took this latter part of Chapter X. to be written by Walton. There is some doubt in my mind as to how much was quoted from that "most honest and excellent Angler" mentioned on page 179 of the fifth edition, and whose initials, B. A., are added at the end of the chapter.

Chapter XI. is a short one on the tench, a fish which Walton tells us " I have not often angled for "; but the baits he recommends I have found to be excellent. The perch, in Chapter XII., and the eel, in Chapter XIII., are well dealt with. Walton gives a quaint reason for being inclined to believe that eels which are bred in rivers connected with the sea never return to fresh water when they have once tasted the salt water, " because I am certain that

powdered [*i.e.*, salted] Beef is a most
excellent bait to catch an eel." In Chapter
XIII. the lamprey, flounder, char, guiniad,
etc., are briefly referred to. The barbel,
as it deserves, has a chapter to itself, for
it "affords an Angler choice sport, being
a lusty and a cunning fish : so lusty and
cunning as to endanger the breaking of
the Angler's line, by running his head
forcibly towards any covert, or hole or
bank : and then striking at the line to
break it off with his tail (as is observed by
Plutarch, in his book *De industria animalium*), and also so cunning to nibble and
suck off your worm close to the hook and
yet avoid the letting the hook come into
his mouth." It would be difficult to find
fault with Walton's directions for fishing
for barbel, or for roach, dace, and other
and smaller fry, which complete the practical portion of his " Discourse " with
Venator. I remember, when I first read
them many years ago, being greatly struck
with one of his methods of taking roach,
and have often found it to be not only a
deadly but also a very interesting one :—

" In many of the hot months, Roaches
may also be caught thus: Take a May-
flie, or Ant-flie, sink him with a little lead
to the bottom, near to the Piles or Posts
of a Bridg, or near to any Posts of a

Weire,—I mean any deep place where Roaches lie quietly, and then pull your flie up very leisurely, and usually a Roach will follow your bait to the very top of the water and gaze on it there, and run at it and take it lest the flie should flie away from him. I have seen this done at Windsor, and Henly Bridg, and great store of Roach taken ; and sometimes a Dace or Chub."

It is most interesting to see a great roach follow the fly up to the surface and "gaze on it," as Walton says.

FISHING-TACKLE MAKERS RECOMMENDED BY WALTON.

In his first edition, page 228, Piscator says to Viator,—

"You must have all these tackling, and twice so many more, with which, if you mean to be a fisher, you must store your-selfe : and to that purpose I will go with you either to *Charles Brandons* (neer to the *Swan* in *Golding-Lane*) ; or to Mr. *Fletchers* in the Court which did once belong to Dr. Nowel the Dean of St. Pauls, that I told you was a good man, and a good Fisher ; it is hard by the west end of Saint Pauls Church ; they be both honest men, and will fit an Angler with what tackling hee wants."

To this Viator replies,—

"'Then, good Master, let it be at *Charles Brandon's*, for he is neerest to my dwelling, and I pray lets meet there the ninth of *May* next about two of the Clock, and I'l want nothing that a Fisher should be furnished with."

In the fifth edition Brandon and Fletcher are not mentioned, and this paragraph is altered thus :—

"And to that purpose I will go with you either to Mr. *Margrave* who dwells amongst the book-sellers in St. *Pauls* Church-Yard, or to Mr. John Stubs, near to the *Swan* in *Golding-Lane*; they be both honest men, and will fit an *Angler* with what *Tackling* he lacks."

At the end of the second part of the fifth edition I find this advertisement :—

" *Courteous Reader,*

"You may be pleas'd to take notice, that at the Sign of the Three Trouts in St. Paul's Church-Yard, on the North side, you may be fitted with all sorts of the best Fishing Tackle, by

"JOHN MARGRAVE."

This modest advertisement must have been invaluable to Margrave; it reads as if drawn up by Walton, who, by the way, has this interesting marginal note on page

237, fifth edition : " *I have heard, that the
tackling hath been prized at fifty pounds in
the Inventory of an Angler.*"

In another place a celebrated hook-
maker is thus referred to :—

" Charles Kirby in Harp Alley in Shoe
Lane, the most exact and best Hook-
maker this nation affords."

Of Fish-Ponds, and How to Order Them.

This is one of the chapters added by
Walton, and is acknowledged by him as
being condensed from Doctor Lebault's
Maison Rustique. Until fresh-water fish
lost much of their value as food for the
people of all classes—that is to say, until
they were superseded by sea fish, much
superior in quality and far more abundant
—the making and ordering of fish-ponds
was of great importance. The number-
less artificial lakes and ponds which exist
in England at the present day owe their
origin in most cases to the great esteem
in which fresh-water fish were formerly
held, especially when our ancestors were
Roman Catholics. In those days they
understood aquaculture far better than we
do, and did not allow their ponds and
lakes to become mere mud-tanks, as is too
often the case now. Walton says :—

"You are to cleanse your Pond, if you intend either profit or pleasure, once every three or four years (especially some ponds), and let it lye dry six or twelve months, both to kill the water weeds, as *Water-lillies*, *Candocks*, *Reate* and *Bull-rushes*, that breed there; and also that as these die for want of water, so grass may grow in the Ponds bottom, which Carps will eat greedily in all the hot months if the Pond be clean."

It is a pity that our landowners of the present day pay so little attention to their ponds and lakes—often for generations they are left untouched, until they hold more mud than water, and are unwholesome for both land and water animals. If they were drained every few years, the mud put on the neighbouring fields, the bottom ploughed and sown with oats, and then used again for breeding fish, they would prove much more profitable than at present. Our farmers forget that the Jews in our large towns are always ready to buy carp and other fresh-water fish with scales: all fish, including eels, have scales; but the Jews will eat only those which have their scales in evidence.

It is also a pity that our farmers do not know that a permanent stream of water running through their land may often be converted into a small gold-mine. A thousand trout fry may be purchased for £5, and if kept for two years will sell for £50—in fact, I have often paid at the rate of two shillings each for them. It is a mistake, also, to suppose that trout will not thrive in still ponds, *if the latter are kept clean.* I always feel sorry for a trout when I see him lying in a few inches of water, with perhaps two or three feet of mud under him instead of the bright gravel he loves so well.

Water from a sewage farm or from sewage-precipitating works ought not to be allowed to flow into our streams. It is quite true fish will live in it, but it is equally true that it causes a rank and noxious growth of flannel and other weeds, and covers the gravelly bed of the stream with a coating of slime. It does not appear to injure the eggs of the coarse fish, roach, dace, etc., as weeds are their natural birth-places, and they hatch out in a few days ; but trout eggs are utterly destroyed, buried under this vegetable slime, long before their hatching period has arrived. It stands to reason that, however clear it may look, sewage water is liquid manure, and as such ought to be turned on to the land—not into the water.

13

To make his work still more "compleat," Walton added to his third and subsequent editions an interesting "Short Discourse by Way of Postscript, touching the Lawes of Angling." Who the writer was is unknown, but he was evidently some learned legal angling friend of Walton, who warmly acknowledges the advantage he has had both from *The Compleat Angler* and the friendship of its author.

One last quotation from Walton's last chapter :—

"*Venator.* Well Master, I thank you for all your good directions, but for none more than this last of thankfulness, which I hope I shall never forget. And pray let's now rest ourselves in this sweet shady Arbour, which Nature herself has woven with her own fine fingers ; 'tis such a contexture of *Woodbines, Sweetbrier, Jessamine,* and *Mirtle* ; and so interwoven, as will secure us both from the Suns violent heat; and from the approaching shower, and being sate down I will requite a part of your courtesies with a bottle of Sack, Milk, Oranges, and Sugar; which all put together, make a drink like Nectar."

A full glass to you, Master ! And may your memory ever be as sweet as "this sweet shady Arbour" of "Woodbines, Sweetbrier, Jessamine, and Mirtle" !

CHAPTER XI.

Some Notes on Charles Cotton's Practical Directions in Trout and Grayling-Fishing—Fish Fine and Far Off—Cotton the First Exponent of Clear-Water Fishing for Trout and Grayling—Yorkshire Fly-Rods—Pike Pool—Creeper-Fishing First Described by Cotton, also "Swimming the Worm" for Grayling.

CHARLES COTTON'S "INSTRUCTIONS HOW TO ANGLE FOR A TROUT OR GRAYLING IN A CLEAR STREAM."

NOW this second part of *The Compleat Angler* came to be written and published has already been noted. I shall here only refer briefly to its practical portions. If Walton was the father of general anglers, Cotton has even greater claims to be considered the first great exponent of clear-water fishing for trout and grayling. I have fished some of his favourite rivers, including the Dove, Derwent, Wye, Bradford, and Lath-

195

kill, or Lathkin, as he calls it; and to appreciate his "Instructions" fully, it is necessary to do so; in fact, it is a duty which every fly-fisher owes to his delightful art to make a pilgrimage to Beresford Dale, Dove Dale, and the other lovely dales and streams of this district. As Walton said in a marginal note on one of Cotton's pages,—

"The pleasantness of the rivers, mountains, and meadows cannot be described, unless Sir Philip Sidney or Mr. Cotton's Father were again alive to do it."

The scene of the "Instructions" is the little fishing-house.

"*Piscator*. Come Boy, set two Chairs, and whilst I am taking a Pipe of Tobacco, which is alwaies my Breakfast, we will, if you please, talk of some other Subject.

*　　*　　*　　*　　*

"*Viator*. I beseech you Sir, do, and if you will lend me your Steel, I will light a Pipe the while, for that is commonly my Breakfast in a morning too."

That Cotton had the confidence born of knowledge appears in his opening lines.

"*Piscator*. Why then Sir, to begin methodically, as a Master in any Art should do (and I will not deny, but that I think myself a Master in this), I shall divide

Angling for Trout or Grayling into these three ways,

At the Top,
At the Bottom, and
In the Middle.

Which three ways, though they are all of them (as I shall hereafter endeavour to make it appear) in some sort common to both those kinds of fish ; yet they are not so generally and absolutely so, but that they will necessarily require a dis-tinction, which in due place I will also give you.

" *That which we call Angling at the Top is with a Flie ;*
" *At the Bottom with a Ground-bait ;*
" *In the Middle with a Minnow, or Ground-bait.*

" Angling at the Top is of two sorts,

With a quick (i.e., live) Flie,
or
With an artificial Flie.

" That we call Angling at the Bottom is also of two sorts,

By hand,
or
With a Cork, or Float.

"That we call Angling in the Middle is also of two sorts,

With a Minnow for a Trout,
or
With a Ground-bait for a Grayling.

"Of all which several sorts of Angling, I will, if you can have the patience to hear me, give you the best account I can."

After this methodical outline Cotton proceeds to describe "Daping, Dabbing, or Dibling" with the natural fly—a fascinating style of fishing still carried on in many parts, notably with the drake on the Irish lakes, where numbers of very heavy fish are taken every May-fly season. On English trout preserves it is not as a rule allowed. In Hartington Mill-Dam I have often seen splendid trout "roving up and down to look for prey," as Cotton says, and doubtless he caught many a good fish there by "daping." He tells us that "many years ago" he had fished in this style with Walton, "one of the best Anglers that ever I knew." As regards fly-rods, he says: "The best that ever I saw are made in Yorkshire, which are all of one piece; that is to say of several, six, eight, ten or twelve pieces, so neatly piec't, and

ty'd together with fine thread below, and
Silk above, as to make it taper, like a
switch, and to ply with a true bent to
your hand ; and these are so light, being
made of Fir wood, for two or three lengths,
nearest to the hand, and of other wood
nearer the top, that a Man might very
easily manage the longest of them that
ever I saw, with one hand."

When fishing on that lovely trout and
salmon river the Eden in Cumberland
some years ago, I found spliced fly-rods of
fir and lance wood were used by many
of the anglers ; and I had one made by
a carpenter at Langwathby who had a
reputation for them.   It was not at all
a bad rod.

As the length of these rods for trout-
fishing is not to be *more* than eighteen feet,
it will be seen that fly-fishers of Cotton's
time could, though no running line was
used, command a good length of line,—
how much he does not say, except to note
that, " to a Man that knows how to handle
his Rod, and to cast, the length of the line
is no manner of encumbrance, excepting
in woody places, and in landing of a Fish,
which every one that can afford to Angle
for pleasure, has some body to do for him,
and the length of line is a mighty advantage
to the fishing at a distance ; and—

To Fish Fine and Far Off is the First and Principal Rule for Trout-Angling.

Your line in this case should never be less, nor ever exceed two hairs next the hook, for one (though some I know will pretend to more Art, than their fellows) is indeed too few, the least accident, with the finest hand being sufficient to break it ; but *he that cannot kill a Trout of twenty inches long with two,* in a River clear of wood and weeds, as this and others of ours are, *deserves not the name of an 'Angler.''*

The words I have italicised in the last paragraph give a standard of skill which any angler of the present day might be proud of, even with our advantage of running line and reel.

Walton acknowledges his indebtedness to Barker for his instructions in fly-making ; and the much more exact and admirable directions given by Charles Cotton were, he tells us on page 51 of his work, " taught me by a kinsman of mine, one Captain Henry Jackson, a near neighbour, an admirable Flie Angler, by many degrees the best Flie Maker, that ever I yet met with."

Here, then, is another angler-soldier of Walton's time to whom we owe something. Cotton and Jackson were Royalists; Colonel Venables and Captain Richard Franck were Cromwellian officers.

What I have never been able to understand is Cotton's calling a grayling " one of the deadest hearted Fishes in the World, and the bigger he is the more easily taken." I have killed a fair share of these beautiful fish in almost every grayling river in this country, and have often found them fight better than a trout, especially in the Test and the Costa. Certainly I have now and then caught a large grayling of 3 lbs. or more which seemed dazed, and instead of fighting rolled over and over helplessly into the net. But, then, who has not had the same experience with a good trout, hooked and got into the net before he realised the situation?

With the fine *undrawn* gut obtainable now we have a far stronger and less apparent means of presenting the fly to the fish than Cotton's double horsehair.

Page 50 of this original edition of Cotton is doubly interesting on account of its containing, not only references to Walton and his son, but also a marginal note by Walton himself.

Piscator Junior, in the course of his practical lesson in fly-fishing, brings his pupil Viator—who, be it remembered, is also the Venator of Walton's " Discourse " —to a scene on the Dove, which causes the visitor to exclaim,—

" *Viator*.   But what have we got here ? A Rock springing up in the middle of the River !   This is one of the oddest sights, that ever I saw.

" *Piscator*.   Why, Sir, from that Pike,* that you see standing up there distant from the Rock, this is call'd Pike-Pool; and young Mr. Izaac Walton was so pleas'd with it, as to draw it in Landscape in black and white in a blank Book I have at home, as he has done several prospects of my house also, which I keep for a memorial of his favour, and will shew you, when we come up to dinner.

* Walton added this marginal note in smaller type: "'Tis a Rock, in the fashion of a Spire-Steeple; and almost as big.   It stands in the midst of the River Dove; and not far from Mr. Cotton's house, below which place this delicate River takes a swift Carere betwixt many mighty Rocks, much higher and bigger than St. Pauls Church, before 'twas burnt.   And this Dove being oppos'd by one of the highest of them, has, at last, forc't itself a way through it; and after a miles concealment, appears again with more glory and beauty than before that opposition ; running through the most pleasant Valleys and most fruitful Meadows, that this Nation can justly boast of."

" *Viator.* Has young Master Izaak Walton been here too?

" *Piscator.* Yes, marry has he Sir, and that again and again too, and in France since, and at Rome, and at Venice, and I can't tell where : but I intend to ask him a great many hard questions so soon as I can see him, which will be, God willing, next month." (Cotton was writing in March 1676.)

An interesting fact, noted first, I think, by Cotton, is that the grayling may be taken in any of the cold months, especially during a frost. He tells us that he " did once take upon the sixt day of December one, and only one, of the biggest Graylings and the best in season, that ever I saw, or tasted . . . and have sometimes in January, so early as New Years-tide, and in frost and snow taken Grayling in a warm sunshine day for an hour or two about noon ; and to fish for him with a grub it is then the best time of all."

The description of flies for use during the season given by Cotton is far ahead of anything which had appeared previously, and for long afterwards remained the standard authority to which fly-fishers referred. Any one who imagines that the flies used more than two hundred years ago were clumsy, large affairs should read Cotton's descriptions carefully : for instance, his dressing of "a very little bright Dun Gnat " on page 55. His chapter on the flies for May is particularly interesting —I mean, of course, to a fly-fisher. His natural history of the stone fly and green drake may not be quite correct in its under-water part, but as an account of what one sees of these insects after their first appearance on the water it is admirable. With an artificial May-fly, Cotton tells us that he once took, between five and eight in the evening, " thirty great Trouts and Graylings, and had no less than five or six Flies with three good hairs apiece taken from me in despite of my heart, besides."

Creeper-fishing in the streamy parts of rivers was first fully described by Cotton, who was also the father of clear-water worm-fishing. That now common expression "Snow Broth " I find first in his book. He, like all the writers of his time, complains bitterly of the poaching then carried on with impunity.

"I assure you, that with this very flie, I have in this very River that runs by us in three or four hours taken thirty, five and thirty, and forty of the best Trouts in the River. What shame and pity is it then, that such a river should be destroyed by the basest sort of people, by those unlawful ways of fire and netting in the night, and of damming, groping, spearing, hanging and hooking by day, which are now grown so common, that, though we have very good Laws to punish such Offenders, every Rascal does it, for ought I see *impuné.*"

Cotton, when mentioning the number of fish he has taken, says "thirty Trouts," instead of " fifteen brace," and it appears at that time to have been the custom in the North to give the full number, and in the South to say so many brace, because in one place (p. 85), where Cotton makes Viator say, " Look you, Sir, here are three brace," Walton has added this note in the margin : "Spoke like a South-Country man."

Stewart and others have claimed for upstream, clear-water worm-fishing, that it is as artistic as, and more difficult than, fly-fishing ; and although whole books have been devoted to this one branch of the sport, I do not think that Cotton's directions have been, or can be, improved upon. He may fairly claim to be the first to fully describe this fascinating style ; he was also the first to note that grayling take a worm swum a foot from the bottom with a cork much better than at the bottom—a style of fishing which Mr. Francis M. Walbran has made popular under the title of " Swimming the Worm." Keen, frosty weather is the time for it, and I hope to have some more pleasant days at it with him on some of Cotton's favourite north-country streams.

Note.—Since I wrote this chapter, in which Cotton's remark about the grayling being a dead-hearted fish is referred to, I took a friend, a salmon and trout-angler, who had never caught a grayling, to the Test: his first fish was one of two pounds, which fought so well and so stubbornly that, when I turned every now and then from my fishing to watch his bending rod, I thought he would have no reason to call a grayling dead-hearted. Later on, among a few brace of good fish I killed, was one of two and a half pounds, which fought splendidly, compelling me to follow him forty yards down stream, and, for a time, spoil one of the best bits of water fishable in a wild November north-easter. I was so warm from the exertion of fishing and playing fish in such a gale, that I did not think of the weather till I noticed the blue nose of my friend the keeper, who was carrying my net: he shivered so that I sent him home.

CHAPTER XII.

SOME EDITIONS OF "THE COMPLEAT ANGLER" SUBSEQUENT TO THE FIFTH.

SO far, in these random casts among the pages of Walton and Cotton, I have had before me copies printed in their time and for them, the very pages of which might have been seen by them. Indeed, as my

207

copy of the fifth edition came from Stafford, it may be one given by Walton to some friend there. In 1714 it belonged to a John Yeomans, who has written his name about it considerably, and in 1715 added this warning :—

"John Yeomans His Booke 1715.

> Steal not this Booke
> for fear of shame
> for hear y see
> the onors name."

Although one may possess, as I do, copies of nearly all the hundred or more of editions of this little work, none can have such a charm for the reader as one of the first five: it adds so infinitely to the interest to know that this old-fashioned type and spelling was every word and letter of it seen by Walton and Cotton, and the collector will always value any one of these most highly.

It is somewhat curious that, although five editions of *The Compleat Angler* were called for between 1653 and 1676, no other edition appeared, or at any rate is known, between that date and 1750, when Moses Browne edited a reprint of it, giving very poor copies of Walton's fish, but adding full-page illustrations by H. Burgh, some of which are, I think, very good, especially that of Trout Hall. The fishing-house must have been drawn from imagination. Browne was the author of *Piscatory Eclogues*, which contain some of the most poetical verses ever written in connection with angling, after those of J. D. There is plenty of verse about our art, but not too much poetry. Browne took the unpardonable liberty of correcting some of the "inaccuracies" and "redundancies" of the original, for which he has been mildly anathematised by Mr. Westwood in his *Chronicle of "The Compleat Angler,"* to which work of more than a hundred pages I would again refer the reader who wishes to get full bibliographical descriptions of the various editions.

Here is a specimen of Browne's verse from an eclogue entitled "Renock's Despair." Renock, "a slighted swain," thus addresses his mistress :—

" O cold as morning dews, as mid-day bright,
  And more than Primrose sweet, than daisy
      white,
  Softer than down that on the thistle grows,
  Which ripe September gives the frolic wind.
  And cruel as the thorn which arms the rose
  Must I unpity'd ever wail my woes,
  Thy lips all pouting, and thy brow severe ;
  While scornful of my fate and abject pains,
  You, to my grief, withhold a soft'ning ear."

14

Not content with making verbal altera-
tions in Walton's text, and improving
some verse which he correctly terms
doggerel, he even tampers with John
Dennys' fine lines quoted by Walton.
Still, his edition has its merits, and his
estimate of Walton and his work is so
true and so well expressed as to make
one regret all the more that he should
have been so unwise as to attempt to
"file off something of that Rust and
Uncouthness, which Time fixes on the
most curious finished Things." He added
a well-compiled appendix of thirty pages,
about rivers, haunts of fish, seasons, tackle,
baits, etc.

Browne's editions of Walton were three
in number: 1750, 1759, and 1772. He
was a friend of Dr. Johnson, who advised
him to publish the work.

Between the second and third issues of
Browne's editions, the first of a much
more notable series appeared—viz., that
edited by John Hawkins in 1760. He
dates the dedication of this edition at
Twickenham, April 10th, 1760, and quite
ignores Moses Browne—except to pat him
on the back for his eclogues. He gave us
the first reliable account of the authors.
But, as I have pointed out at some length
in my "Lea and Dove" edition of *The*

Compleat Angler, it was to that indefatigable antiquary William Oldys, Norroy
King-at-Arms, that we owe the principal
facts about Walton and Cotton which have
come down to us, and not to Sir John
Hawkins, to whom they have been in-
variably credited. Mr. Thoms, when
editor of *Notes and Queries*, was the first,
I believe, to point out how much we owe
to Oldys.

The illustrations of fish in Hawkins's
edition, although better than Browne's, are
still much inferior to those in Walton's
first edition. The copper-plate full-page
views of scenes described in the book
were engraved by Ryland from designs by
Wale. Browne complained, and not without justice, I think, that some of these
illustrations came near being copies of
those in his book. If S. Wale, Jun., had
not seen the picture of the anglers lunch-
ing under the sycamore tree in Browne's
edition, or that of the meeting between
them and the milkmaid and her mother,
it is difficult to account for the similarity
between his designs and those of Burgh.
The plates of music are beautifully engraved in Hawkins, as one would expect
from the author of *A History of Music*,
and he added some most useful engravings of tackle, including a winch, of

methods of splicing rods, of aquatic insects, artificial flies, etc. He also added considerably to the "Short Discourse by way of Postscript touching the Laws of Angling," which was published first with the third edition of the *Angler*. He also gave in an appendix an extended list of flies and their dressings—some, I expect, from Bowlker. Above all, he reproduced Walton's text carefully. The first edition was printed for Thomas Hope, 1760; the second for J. Rivington, 1766; and the third for John and Francis Rivington, 1775; and, in 1784, the last edition published during the lifetime of the editor, with some additions, was published by John, Francis, and Charles Rivington.

Passing over two further editions in the Hawkins series, published with a few notes by his son, we come to the first Bagster edition, 1808. This, as Mr. Westwood says, is the "tallest" edition published up to that time. I have a fine copy of it before me. The illustrations are, as regards the fishing scenes, copies of those in Hawkins re-engraved by Philip Audinet, who also did the fish, which are for the most part a vast improvement on anything in Hawkins. With reference to these illustrations, the

publisher, in a note dated 81, Strand,
1808, says that those which were previously used are not copied from the
old plates, but re-engraved from the
original drawings of Mr. Wale; that "the
sketch of Mr. Cotton's fishing-house, and
the view of Pike-pool, having been found
inaccurate, Mr. Samuel has favoured the
publisher with a finished drawing of Pike-
pool, and a sketch of the fishing-house
taken by himself on the spot in the year
1799. Nor are the engravings of Fishes
copied from the plates of any preceding
edition ; they are, in general, actual portraits of Fish which have been recently
captured."

Portraits of Walton, Cotton, Hawkins,
Wotton, Hooker, Herbert, and Dr. Donne
are given ; and in the Life of Walton some
additional particulars are added on the
authority of Dr. Zouch, who in 1790 had
also published a Life.

This Bagster edition was in point of
fact a reissue of Hawkins's with embellish-
ments, the new view of the fishing-house
being one of the best. It is an edition
much prized by collectors, in its octavo,
royal octavo, and quarto forms. One
collector, whose name was Higgs, had
a copy specially bound, the bands of
the book being made with wood from the

door of Cotton's fishing-house, taken off
by Higgs near the lock, "where he was
sure old Izaak's hand must have touched
it." This copy afterwards sold for £63.
Walton's coffin would not be safe from
some of his "admirers."

The second Bagster-Hawkins edition
appeared in 1815, with some notes by
Sir Henry Ellis, of the British Museum,
and new plates of fish. This edition was
a great favourite with Mr. Westwood,
being the first in which he read Walton.
It was printed by R. Watts, of Broxbourne,
on the River Lea, Herts.

In 1822 Thomas Gosden reprinted
Hawkins's edition with a new set of plates,
which "did triple duty, they being offered
for sale in a separate shape, and employed
to illustrate the reprint of Zouch's Life of
Walton, published by Gosden in 1823,
and subsequently." Mr. Westwood, I
think, scarcely does justice to the illustrations in Gosden's edition. There is one of
a group of fish from an original picture by
Elmer "in the possession of the publisher,"
in which is one of the best illustrations of
a trout ever published. The engravings
of the fishing-house, of Beresford Hall,
of Walton's house in Fleet Street, etc.,
are also excellent, and are certainly not
"anachronisms,"—if the same can be said

of the fishing scenes. By notes and
appendices the information of Walton was
supposed to be brought down to date ; and
I fail to see why, in introducing modern
fishing scenes, or what were modern in
1822, Gosden should be charged with
inserting "anachronisms" scarcely in
unison with the quaint character of the
book. Indeed, from a picture of "King
Charles II. in disguise in the Oak,"
published during Walton's lifetime, I am
inclined to think that the ordinary every-
day costume of the angler in his time was
nearer to that of 1822 than as depicted
by Burgh, for instance, in Moses Browne's
edition.

Again, as regards the plates being used
for more than one book, I fear most of
the illustrations which have been made
for most of the editions of Walton have
been "hashed up" over and over again.
Take the next "new issue" of the *Angler*
—Major's, in 1823. Major's illustrations
have been constantly reprinted or copied,
either wholly or in part, into new editions ;
which is certainly a compliment to Major,
but somewhat disappointing to the collector.

While doing full justice to the beauty
of Major's editions, especially that of 1844,
Mr. Westwood lashes him for his vanity

in writing an essay on Walton. " In one passage he attempts to gloss over Walton's humble position in early life, and establish a claim for consideration, not so much on his own intrinsic merits, as on the ground of his high relations and fine acquaintances—a piece of snobbishness which draws on him the justly indignant rebuke of Dr. Bethune."

Major's first edition contained the old designs by Wale which had figured so often before—" greatly heightened in the effect by the pencil of Mr. Frederick Nash " and engraved by Cook and Pye—and very good woodcuts of fish. In his second edition (1824) the fourteen copper-plates were re-engraved by W. R. Smith. His third edition was in 1835, and his last edition (*i.e.*, the last issued by him) in 1844. Mr. Westwood says of this edition : " It was printed, as before, in two sizes—crown and royal octavo. The obnoxious "Introductory Essay " still sticks to the work like a burr ; but with this remark our censure exhausts itself ; in other respects the volume approaches more nearly to our ideal of an edition consistent in all its parts than any of its predecessors or successors. Wale's designs, repeated *ad nauseam*, are here suppressed, and a new series by Absolon substituted, embodying the same subjects, but conceived in no plagiaristic spirit."

Certainly the 1844 Major is an edition of Walton which every collector and lover of Walton is glad to possess. He tells us that "the new designs by Absolon form the crown of my present efforts." Absolon's nine drawings were engraved by J. T. Willmore, A.R.A. There are seventy-four woodcuts in the text, many of them being charming views of scenery by T. Creswick, A.R.A. Major says in one place : "I had long been asking myself, in the language of Abraham Cowley, 'What shall I do to be for ever known?' And my good Genius whispered, 'Give your days and nights to *emblazon* the worth of Izaak Walton.'" What would Major have said if he could have seen the numerous editions which have to thank his "emblazonments" for their existence—not always with acknowledgments to him ?

But between the first and fourth Majors appeared other editions of Walton, including Pickering's *magnum opus*, and an edition of which no trace can be found. This, Mr. Westwood says, is described in the London Catalogue, 1815-1832, as a 6s. foolscap 8vo reprint by Maunder in 1824. I would give something for an edition of Walton of which Mr. Westwood

could say all his efforts to obtain a copy
had proved abortive.

Among the editions I have of Walton,
one I prize greatly is the smallest of all,
a little 32mo—Pickering's first edition in
1825. This wee volume, little more than
three inches long, two wide, and half
an inch thick, contains the whole of
Walton and Cotton, uncumbered by
notes. The type is small, but the whole
goes into a watch-pocket, and my copy
has travelled with me many thousands
of miles.

But Pickering is not represented alone
by the smallest Walton in existence. He
gave us also in some respects the finest
and most valuable, that of 1836—the
" result of seven years' continuous labour
and of much patient research and fostering
care on the part of its publisher." This
edition is in two imperial 8vo volumes.
The editor was Sir Harris Nicolas, the
most indefatigable and careful editor that
Walton ever had. What Sir Harris
Nicolas has said leaves, as Mr. Westwood
notes, " little in the way of *data* for any
future gleaner in the same scanty field."
"The illustrators are Stothard and Inskipp, the former being charged with
the scenic plates and the views of the
localities, and the latter, principally, with

the fish." I confess I do not agree with the estimate of this edition formed by Mr. Westwood. He does not care for Stothard's illustrations, calls them unworthy of the book and of the artist, but admits that Inskipp's fish, "with some exceptions," display all the force and freshness of nature. I think that if you want Walton with editorial annotation developed to its utmost limits, with scenic and other illustrations to match, you must have this third edition of Pickering.

Among the American reprints of Walton, that of Dr. Bethune, first published in 1847, is far and away the best. The *Chronicle* pays it this high compliment— " For the lover of angling books, and for the collector especially, there is no edition so useful as this"; and quotes the following reference to it in Mr. J. Wynne's *Private Libraries of New York* :—

" During the darker seasons of the year, when forbidden the actual use of his rod, our friend has occupied himself with excursions through sale catalogues, fishing out from their dingy pages whatever tends to honour his favourite author and favourite art, so that his spoils now number nearly five hundred volumes of all sizes and dates. Pains have been taken to have, not only copies of the works included by the list, but also the several editions, and when it is of a work mentioned by Walton, an edition which the good old man himself may have seen."

Difficult, indeed, would it be to find anything in *The Compleat Angler* which has not been "annotated" in some form or other. In an "interview" with Mr. Harting about his forthcoming edition, I see he is made to say that Walton's mistake about the cuttle-fish, in confounding it with the "Angler" or "Devil" fish, has escaped notice. I think, if he refers to Dr. Bethune's edition, page 38, he will find he is mistaken :—

"'The cuttle-fish, which is not properly a fish, but of the class Mollusca, is confounded here with the *Lophius piscatorius*, common angler, toad-fish, sea-frog, sea-devil."

Dr. Bethune's edition is certainly one which every collector should possess, not for its beauty of typography or illustration, but for the collection of information about Walton, and the "cordial, reverent and sympathetic" criticism of its editor. There have been several reprints of Dr. Bethune's edition. In 1880 a reissue appeared in New York by John Wiley & Sons, in 2 vols., demy 8vo, with this note :—

"From the Publisher to the Reader.

" In putting forth this edition of Walton and Cotton, the original (Bethune) text of 1847 has been strictly adhered to, except where the marginal notes which Dr. Bethune added to his own private copy corrected an error, or added information which at the time of its first publication he had not acquired."

In 1891 Messrs. Ward, Lock, & Co. reissued this edition in one volume.

In 1853 appeared the first of the " Ephemera" editions of Walton. " Ephemera" was the *nom de plume* of Edward Fitzgibbon, for many years the angling editor of *Bell's Life in London*, and author of some excellent books on fishing. He was a thoroughly practical angler, and in piles of notes corrected and brought down to date the " Instructions" of Walton. His editions, first published by Ingram & Cooke, and afterwards by Routledge, being cheap, have had a large sale.

A German Edition of Walton.

It is perhaps unfortunate that the edition of such an iconoclastic editor as " Ephemera" should have been selected

for translation into the only edition of
Walton into a foreign language that has
appeared. "Ephemera" seems to have
set Walton up in order to knock him down.
He is like a good-humoured, but often
irate, schoolmaster, "lecturing" a scholar
for his mistakes, and then putting him
right in a solemn and lengthy manner.
His edition, with his voluminous notes,
was translated into German by T. Schu-
macherr, and published in 1859, with
illustrations by P. Salomon & Co., of
Hamburg, under the title of

"DER VOLLKOMMENE ANGLER."

After a good deal of advertising in
Germany, I succeeded in obtaining a copy,
and find that, as well as "Ephemera's"
notes, many of those by Sir John Hawkins
are also translated, and some by the trans-
lator added. But what could a German
reader be expected to think of Walton
when the German publisher apologises
for a "certain heaviness" in him "which
could not be avoided in the translation,"
and the editor continually corrects the
author in this style ?—

"Dieser Kurze Paragraph enthält be-
trübende Irrthümer.

"Dieser Paragraph und der vorher-

gehende sind mit blühendem und hand-
greiflichem Unsinn angefüllt."

The translation is evidently carefully,
if not always correctly done, and that is
all that can be said for it. It is common-
place and heavy. It was a bold undertaking to attempt to translate Walton.
"Ephemera's" notes are admirably rendered, but all the spirit of *The Compleat
Angler* is missing.

I give one or two specimens.

THE COMPLEAT ANGLER.	DER VOLKOMMENE ANGLER.
Second Day.	*Zweiter Tag.*
"*Ven.* My friend Piscator, you have kept time with my thoughts, for the Sun is just rising, and I my self just now come to this place, and the dogs have just now put down an Otter. Look down at the bottom of the hill there in that meadow, chequered with Water-Lillies and Lady-smocks, there you may see what work they make; look, look! you may see all busie, men and dogs, dogs and men, all busie.	"*Ven.* Mein Freund Piscator, unsere Gedanken haben sich gekreuzt, denn die Sonne ist gerade im Aufgehen begriffen, ich selbst bin erst eben angekommen, und in diesen Augenblicke haben die Hunde eine Otter gefangen. Blicken Sie hügelabwärts nach jener, mit Wasserlilien und Wiesenblumen besäten Wiese, dann werden Sie sehen, was schon gethan ist. Sehen Sie wie Männer und Hunde, Hunde und Männer alle thätig sind.

" *Pisc.* Sir, I am right glad to meet you, and glad to have so fair an entrance into this dayes sport, and glad to see so many dogs, and more men all in pursuit of the Otter; lets complement no longer, but joyn unto them; come, honest *Venator*, lets be gone, let us make hast; I long to be doing: no reasonable hedg or ditch shall hold me."

" *Pisc.* Ich bien wahrhaftig sehr erfreut Sie getroffen zu haben, und einer so angenehmen Eröffnung der Jagd beizuwohnen, aber am meisten erfreut es mich, so viele Männer und Hunde in Verfolgung der Otter begriffen zu sehen. Lassen sie uns keine Zeit mit Reden verschwenden, sondern uns sofort der Jagd ansschlieszen. Kommen Sie, mein ehrenwerther Venator, beeilen wir uns, und machen wir, dasz wir fortkommen, ich sehne mich danach thätig mitzuwirken; keine Hecke, kein Teich soll uns aufhalten."

In German, Piscator requires far longer words and more of them to reply to Venator, who has, moreover, knocked all the spirit out of the thing by telling his friend that the dogs have *caught* the otter, whereas, of course, the sport had only just commenced.

Nearly all the verses in Walton are translated, with Coridon's catches and the milkmaid's songs, all in a straightforward and matter-of-fact, business-like manner.

One verse of Herbert's lines will be
enough :—

"Sweet day. so cool, so calm, so bright,
    The bridal of the earth and skie ;
Sweet dews shall weep thy fall to-night,
        For thou must die."

" O ! kühler Tag, der heiter lacht,
    Als ob die Erde Hochzeit hab' ;
Es weint um Dich der Thau bei Nacht,
        Du sinkst in's Grab."

There are some very pretty fishing scenes
in the Walton edited by Jesse and published by Bohn in 1856, with reprints
in 1870 and 1876.

The *Chronicle* has, I am glad so see,
a good word for the edition published by
Bell & Daldy and Low in 1863, to which
I have referred in the Introduction to this
little volume. In 1866 and 1867 Messrs.
Little, Brown, & Co., of Boston, U.S.A.,
published a reproduction of the best of
Major's editions, the 1844. "The woodcuts were re-engraved for this edition, and
are held to be finer than those employed
in the English issue." The steel engravings are from the original plates. In
1876 Mr. Elliot Stock published a
facsimile reprint of the first edition,
published in 1653. Seeing that it was
published when photographic processes
had not been brought to such perfection

15

as at present, I think the illustrations hardly deserve the censure meted out to them in the *Chronicle*.

In 1888 I brought out the " Lea and Dove" edition, being the hundredth edition of *The Compleat Angler*, in two volumes, small quarto, and a limited large-paper edition. My idea was to make illustrations of scenes on the rivers Lea and Dove the leading feature of this issue, and to give the text of the old classic in a style worthy, if possible, of its hundredth edition, and entirely unencumbered with notes. The text was printed from new type by Messrs. William Clowes & Sons, Limited, who took the greatest interest in the work. The illustrations consist of about one hundred small woodcuts and fifty full-page photo-engraved plates of views on the Lea and Dove—those on the Lea by Mr. P. H. Emerson, B.A., and those on the Dove by Mr. George Bankart. Possessors of this edition may at any rate rest satisfied that it will not be reprinted, as the copper-plates I had transformed into boxes for keeping fly-books free from moth, and the type has been distributed. Of the reception of this edition both by the Press and the public I will only say that I was more than satisfied.

It is pleasant to note the number of

editions of Walton which bear the imprint
of American publishers, chiefly, of course,
reprints of English editions or editions
printed in England. The most beautiful
edition we have had from America was
one published in 1889 in two octavo
volumes by Little, Brown, & Co., of Boston
(London, Macmillan & Co.), with a small
large-paper edition, of which I was glad
to secure a copy, both because of the fact
that it contains an " Introduction," extending to over fifty pages, by no less a
writer than Mr. James Russell Lowell, and
for the etchings by Harlow, which have
been added to the illustrations from
Major's edition of 1844, with some fish
by Inskipp from the great Pickering
edition of 1836. I must refer to Mr.
Lowell's "Introduction" in another chapter.

Before closing these brief notes about
some of the more prominent of the many
editions of Walton, I must put in a word
of welcome for yet another. I have received from Messrs. Samuel Bagster &
Sons, Limited, the prospectus of an *édition
de luxe* of *The Compleat Angler* to be published shortly, " Edited, with Notes from
a Naturalist's Point of View," by Mr. J. E.
Harting, Librarian to the Linnæan Society
of London, editor of *The Zoologist*, and
author of many delightful works about

birds. There are to be new illustrations of riverside animals and birds by Mr. G. C. Lodge ; also fifty illustrations by Percy Thomas. Two volumes, small quarto, of three hundred pages each. As already noted, Samuel Bagster's name as a publisher of editions of Walton is well known to collectors. I have some "tall copies" of them dated before this century was in its teens.

Note.—*In consequence of the "earthquake" mentioned in a previous chapter, I find I had omitted to mention an edition of Walton which all collectors ought to have: I refer to that edited by Captain H. J. Alfred, published by W. H. Allen & Co. in 1885, with copious notes by well-known members of the Gresham and other angling societies, etc.*

CHAPTER XIII.

Lines to Walton Published in 1619—Letters and References to Him by the Bishops of Chichester, Winchester, Lincoln, and the Archbishop of Canterbury—Sir Henry Wotton's Letter to Walton—The Commendatory Verses Prefixed to *The Compleat Angler*—Drayton and Ben Jonson—Dr. Johnson and Walton—An Extract from *The American Review*, 1830—Sir Walter Scott's Reference to Walton and Franck's *Northern Memoirs*—Some Extracts from James Russell Lowell's "Introduction" to an Edition of the *Angler*—Conclusion.

SOME CONTEMPORARY AND SUBSEQUENT OPINIONS ABOUT WALTON AND "THE COMPLEAT ANGLER."

"There are them that have left a name behinde them ; so that their praise shall be spoken of."—ECCLUS. xliv. 8.*

IN the following pages I give a few of the many references to Walton and his work, which show in what esteem he has always been held both during and after his life.

* This quotation was placed by Walton on the title-page of his *Life of Sir Henry Wotton*,

229

It is to Mr. J. Payne Collier we owe the discovery of the first reference to Walton. He pointed out, in his *Poetical Decameron*, that a short poem, entitled *The Love of Amos and Laura*, by S. P., published in 1619, is dedicated thus :—

"TO MY APPROVED AND MUCH-RE-SPECTED FRIEND, IZ. WA.

" To thee, thou more than thrice-beloved friend,
    I, too unworthy of so great a bliss,
These harsh-tun'd lines I here to thee com-
        mend,
    Thou being cause it is now as it is ;
For had'st thou held thy tongue, by silence
        might
These have been buried in oblivious night.

" If they were pleasing I would call them thine,
    And disavow my title to the verse,
But being bad, I needs must call them mine,
    No ill thing can be clothed in thy verse.
Accept them then, and where I have offended,
Rase thou it out and let it be amended."

The S. P. whose initials are attached to this poem is supposed to have been Samuel Purchas, author of *The Pilgrimage*, and other poems.

One of Walton's earliest friends in London was the celebrated Dr. Donne. He was his parishioner when Donne was

sometime Provost of Eaton Colledge, published by Richard Marriot in 1670.

vicar of St. Dunstan's, and it is probable that through him he was introduced to so many of the leading clergy and men of letters of his day. For instance, writing in the year 1664, Dr. King, Lord Bishop of Chichester, thus addresses Walton.

EXTRACTS FROM THE LETTERS OF DR. KING, THE BISHOP OF CHICHESTER, AND OTHER CHURCHMEN TO WALTON.

"HONEST ISAAC,*—Though a familiarity of more than Forty years continuance, and the constant experience of your Love even in the worst times, be sufficient to indear our Friendship; yet, I must confess my Affection much improved, not only by Evidences of Private Respect to many that know and love you, but by your new Demonstration of a publick Spirit, testified in a diligent, true, and useful Collection of so many Material Passages as you have now afforded me in the Life of Venerable Mr. Hooker." . . .

The letter goes on to remind Walton that he was present at Donne's bedside three days before his death, to commend his Lives of Donne and Sir Henry Wotton,

* Both by his friends and himself Walton's name is written as "Izaak" and "Isaac." I have copied it as I found it.

and to give him some information about the " ever memorable Mr. Hooker," and proceeds :—

" Lastly, I must again congratulate this Undertaking of yours, as now more proper to you than to any other person, by reason of your long Knowledge and Alliance to the worthy Family of the Cranmers (my old Friends also). . . . And let me say further; you merit much from many of Mr. Hooker's best Friends then living, namely, from the ever renowned Archbishop Whitgift, of whose incomparable worth, with the character of the Times, you have given us a more short and significant account than I have received from any other Pen." . . .

The Bishop signs himself:—

" One who heartily wishes your happiness, and is unfainedly,

"Sir,

" Your ever-faithful and

" Affectionate old Friend,

" HENRY CHICHESTER.

"CHICHESTER, *November* 17*th*, 1664."

In the same letter the Bishop tells Walton that "Mr. John Hales * (of Eaton College) affirm'd to me he had not seen

* "Our Bibliotheca ambulans" Sir Henry Wotton calls him.

a Life written with more advantage to the
Subject, or more reputation to the Writer,
than that of Dr. Donne's."

This testimony from an experience of
"more than forty years" to the worth of
Walton is written by Bishop King, and
prefixed to the first collected edition of
Walton's Lives of Donne, Wotton, Hooker,
and Herbert, published in 1670 by
Richard Marriot, and dedicated to Dr.
George Morley, Bishop of Winchester.
In the course of this dedication, Walton
says that his Lives of Herbert and Donne
were written under Bishop Morley's roof,
and that if it has been possible for him
to make his Lives "passable in an
eloquent and captious age, it is by the
advantage of forty years friendship, and
thereby the hearing of and discoursing
with your Lordship."

This, then, is another forty years' testimony.

In his "Epistle to the Reader" published
with this 1670 edition of the Lives, Walton
tells us that Doctor Gilbert Sheldon,
afterwards Archbishop of Canterbury, had
"twice injoyn'd" him to write the Life of
Hooker. Dr. Sheldon was, he tells us in
his *Angler*, a very skilful angler for barbel.

Sir William Dugdale, in his *Short View
of the Late Troubles in England*, refers to

the " great judgment and integrity " with which Walton had compiled the Life of Hooker.

In his " Epistle Dedicatory " of his Life of Dr. Sanderson, Bishop of Lincoln, Walton, addressing Dr. George Morley, Bishop of Winchester, thanks him for having introduced him to " Dr. Sanderson, Mr. Chillingworth and Dr. Hammond," men whose merits ought never to be forgotten ; and he mentions that his friendship for Dr. Sanderson " was begun almost forty years past."

The Bishop of Lincoln, dating his letter London, May 10th, 1678, thus addresses Walton :—

" MY WORTHY FRIEND MR. WALTON,— I am heartily glad that you have undertaken to write the Life of that excellent person, and (both of learning and piety) eminent Prelate, Dr. Sanderson, late Bishop of Lincoln ; because I know your ability to know, and integrity to write truth."

After furnishing some particulars about Sanderson asked for by Walton, he concludes thus :—

" Pray pardon this rude, and I fear, impertinent scribble, which (if nothing else) may signify thus much, that I am willing to obey your desires, and am indeed

"Your affectionate Friend

"THOMAS LINCOLN.

"LONDON, *May 10th*, 1678."

We see from these brief extracts that Walton was personally known to, and beloved by,—

Dr. Henry King, Bishop of Chichester;

Dr. George Morley, Bishop of Winchester;

Dr. Gilbert Sheldon, Archbishop of Canterbury;

Dr. Robert Sanderson, Bishop of Lincoln;

Dr. Thomas Barlow, Bishop of Lincoln.

SIR HENRY WOTTON TO HIS "WORTHY FRIEND."

On February 27th, 1672, Walton wrote a dedication of the fourth edition of his *Reliquiæ Wottonianæ* to the Right Honourable Philip, Earl of Chesterfield, who was a grand-nephew of Sir Henry Wotton, in which I find he says that two of his reasons for dedicating the work to his lordship were,—

1. "That Sir Henry Wotton, whose many merits made him an Ornament, even

to your Family, was yet so humble, as to acknowledge me to be his Friend; and died in a belief that I was so.

2. "My other reason of this boldness, is, an incouragement (very like a command) from your worthy Cousin, and my Friend, Mr. Charles Cotton."

Among the *Reliquiæ Wottonianæ* are "Letters to several Persons," including Lord Bacon, Milton, and Walton. In one "To Iz. Wa., In answer of a Letter requesting him to perform his promise of writing the Life of Dr. Donne," which is not dated, but from the closing lines was evidently written in the spring, Sir Henry Wotton says:—

"My Worthy Friend,—I am not able to yield any reason, no, not so much as may satisfie myself, why a most ingenuous Letter of yours hath lain so long by me (as it were in Lavender) without an Answer, save this only, The pleasure I have taken in your Style and Conceptions, together with a Meditation of the subject you propound, may seem to have cast me into a gentle slumber. But being now awaked, I do herein return you most hearty thanks for the kind prosecution of your 1st motion, touching a just Office, due to the memory of our ever memorable

Friend: To whose good fame though it be needless to add anything, (and my age considered almost hopeless from my pen;) yet I will endeavour to perform my promise, if it were but even for this cause, that in saying somewhat of the Life of so deserving a man, I may perchance over-live mine own.

"That which you add of Doctor King (now made Dean of Rochester, and by that translated into my native soil) is a great spur unto me; with whom I hope shortly to confer about it in my passage towards Boughton Malherb, (which was my genial Air) and invite him to a friendship with that Family where his Predecessor was familiarly acquainted. I shall write you at large by the next messenger, (being at present a little in Business) and then I shall set down certain general Heads, wherein I desire Information by your loving Diligence; hoping shortly to enjoy your own ever welcome Company in this approaching time of the *Fly* and the *Cork.* And so I rest

"Your very hearty poor Friend
to serve you,
"H. Wotton."

In another letter Sir Henry tells Walton that since he last saw him he had been

confined to his chamber by a "quotidian
Fever producing those Splenetick Vapours
that are called *Hypochondriacal*; of which
most say, the Cure is good Company; and
I desire no better Physician than yourself."

Among Wotton's poems in this collection are the pleasant lines quoted in
The Compleat Angler, entitled "On a
Bank as I sate a-Fishing," of which the
first eight lines run,—

> "And now all Nature seem'd in Love,
>   The lusty Sap began to move;
> New Juice did stir th' embracing Vines,
> And Birds had drawn their Valentines:
> The jealous Trout, that low did lie,
> Rose at a well-dissembled Flie:
> There stood my Friend, with patient skill
> Attending of his trembling Quill."

After pleasant wading through this
thick volume of seven hundred pages, this
is all I can find referring to Walton; but
it is ample for my purpose. Sir Henry
Wotton died in November 1639, before
Walton had published anything except
perhaps an elegy or two; and yet Walton
must have been for many years before
that his esteemed friend and angling
companion.

The "Commendatory Verses."

It is somewhat curious that although

the first edition of the *Angler* was published in 1653, the second, published in
1655, contained commendatory verses
from seven of Walton's friends not in the
first, although one of these addresses,
" To the Readers of my most ingenuous
Friends Book, *The Compleat Angler*,"
written by Edward Powel, M.A., is dated
April 3rd, 1650.

In these verses the writer refers to
Walton's "matchless Lives of Donne and
Wotton "; "but the latter was not published until 1651, so that there appears to
be a mistake in a date ; and yet "April 3rd,
1650," appears again with Powel's verses
in the fifth edition in 1676, and surely
would have been corrected had it been
an error of the printer.

Hear what these friends of Walton say
in a few extracts from their lines :—

" To the Reader of ' The Compleat Angler.'

" First mark the Title well; my friend that gave it
   Has made it good ; this book deserves to
      have it.
For he that views it with judicious looks,
Shall find it full of art, baits, lines and hooks.
The world the river is ; both you and I,
And all mankind, are either fish or fry :
If we pretend to reason, first or last
His baits will tempt us, and his hooks hold
      fast."
                              CH. HARVIE, M.A.

Then follow some verses dated 1649, addressed, "To my dear Friend Mr. Iz. Walton, in praise of Angling, which we both love," by Tho. Weaver, M.A.

"*To the Readers of my most ingenuous Friends Book 'The Compleat Angler.'*"

"He that both knew and writ the lives of men, Such as were once, but must not be agen;

. . . .

Reader, this He, this Fisherman comes forth, And in these Fishers weeds would shroud his worth."

EDW. POWEL, M.A., *April 3rd*, 1650.

"*To my dear Brother, Mr. Iz. Walton, on his 'Compleat Angler.'*"

"This Book is so like you and you like it, For harmless Mirth, Expression, Art and Wit, That I protest ingenuously 'tis true, I love this Mirth, Art, Wit, the Book and You."

ROB. FLOUD.

"Clarissimo amicissimoque Fratri, Domino Isaaco Walton, Artis Piscatoriæ peritissimo."

HENRY BAYLEY, M.A.

"*Ad Virum optimum & Piscatorem peritissimum, Isaacum Waltonum.*"

The first two lines of this long Ode run :—

"Magister artis docte Piscatoriæ, Waltone Salve, magne dux arundinis."

J. D.

JAMES DUPORT, D.D., [*Greek Professor at Cambridge, evidently an angler, as in another Ode to Walton he says,*—]

"Næ tu Magister, et ego discipulus tuus,
(Nam candidatum & me ferunt arundinis)."

I have given some other charming lines by Duport, written in a book he gave to Walton, among the "Waltoniana" of the "Lea and Dove" edition.

Sir Richard Baker, author of *The Chronicle of the Kings of England*, who refers to Dr. Donne and Sir Henry Wotton as "two of mine own old acquaintance," says, "The Trojan horse was not fuller of heroic Grecians, than King James's reign was full of men excellent in all kinds of learning."

From the brief extracts I have given, we see that Walton was the esteemed friend of some of the best of these contemporaries. He speaks of Drayton as his "honest old friend." He knew Ben Jonson, and at the end of some particulars about him which he gave Aubrey he says, "So much for brave Ben."

DR. SAMUEL JOHNSON AND WALTON.

It is interesting and significant of Walton's worth as a writer, that the literary giant of the next century, Johnson, should have advised the publication of a new edition of *The Compleat Angler*, when that work had been out of print for nearly a century, also that he should have contemplated writing a Life of Walton.

Moses Browne, in the Preface to his edition of Walton's *Angler*, says he undertook it " at the invitation of a very ingenious and learned friend (Mr. Samuel Johnson), who mentioned to me, I remember, in that Conversation his Design to write the Life of Walton. I wish he had performed it." Boswell tells us that Johnson " talked of Isaac Walton's Lives, which was one of his most favourite books. Dr. Donne's Life, he said, was the most perfect of them."

Moses Browne gives his estimate of the book in these enthusiastic words :—

" Mr. Isaack Walton's *Compleat Angler* has been always had in greatest reputation, by such as are acquainted with Books, and have any Discernment, in works of Merit and Nature. And is so happy to have this which is very singular and uncommon to recommend it, that it has found the Way to make itself exceedingly agreeable to Readers of all Tastes, who have perused it. Not only the lovers of this Art, but all others that have least inclination to the Diversion it treats of,

have join'd in giving it their mutual Commendation. . . . Its suitable unaffected
Negligence and Simplicity of style, the
hardest to imitate; and almost peculiar
to himself, enlivened natural Descriptions,
the many curious Discoveries (for its Time)
in matters of philosophical and historical
Science, the happiest mixture of religious
and moral Instruction, enlivened with a
vein of innocent Humour, and chearful
entertainment appear in every page of it."

But it would be impossible to make
note of all the references to Walton.
D'Israeli, I remember, somewhere speaks
of his " Doric Sweetness "; Wordsworth,
of " Meek Walton's heavenly memory."
Dr. Zouch, as Sir Harris Nicolas says,
"has almost exhausted panegyric in his
praises of Walton."

FROM "THE AMERICAN REVIEW," 1830.

One of the most interesting references
I have come across is the following, from
the Life by Sir Harris Nicolas :—

" There is much that the admirers of
Walton will read with pleasure in a
criticism which appeared in *The American
Review* of the Diary of Wilson, the
ornithologist.   Wilson says :—

" ' 1810, *April* 25.—Breakfasted at

Walton's, thirteen miles from Nashville. The hospitable landlord, Isaac Walton, upon setting out early the next morning, refused to take anything for my fare; saying, "You seem to be travelling for the good of the world, and I cannot, I will not charge you anything; whenever you come this way, call and stay with me— you shall be welcome." This is the first instance of such hospitality which I have met with in the United States.'

"On this passage the American Reviewer observes :—

"'Upon reading this note, our faith in the doctrine of Pythagoras grew strong. Can it be that the soul of that gentle parent of the angle, old Izaak Walton, in winging its terrestrial flight from the margin of the sea, found a kindred tenement in mine excellent host of Tennessee ? We fear poor Wilson never luxuriated over the verdant pages of that golden book, *The Compleat Angler*, or he would have anticipated our passing tribute to its author. We too had, peradventure, died in ignorance, had it not been pointed out to us by the venerable author of *The Man of Feeling*, himself a brother of the gentle craft. We recall the era of the event as one of the greenest spots both in our literary and piscatory existence, and have ever since held it a settled maxim of our belief, in defiance of which we are ready to do battle, that no brother of the angle can by any possibility prove a recreant.'" *

SIR WALTER SCOTT AND WALTON.

I daresay it would not be difficult to find a good many writers who, like Landor, gently scoff at Walton (see his "Imaginary Conversation" between Walton, Cotton, and Oldways), or, like his contemporary Captain Franck, who, in his *Northern Memoirs*, tells us he met Walton at Stafford, and that because he offered Walton a very probable natural solution of some supernatural statement he (Walton) had quoted from Gesner, Walton went off in a huff. To judge from his book, I should say it was far more likely Walton, if he was "huff'd" at all, was so by Franck's "affected pedantry" and "stupendous pretentiousness" There has been only one reprint of Franck's book (which was written in Walton's lifetime—in fact, in 1658, though not published till 1685, two years after Walton's death), and the author must have turned in his grave when the reprint was published; for its

* *The American Review*, No. xvi., December 1830, p. 376. I wonder who was editor of *The American Review* at this time?—R. B. M.

editor, Sir Walter Scott, in his Introduction, says :—

" Probably no reader, while he reads the disparaging passages in which the venerable Isaac Walton is introduced, can forbear wishing that the good old man, who had so true an eye for Nature, so simple a taste for her most innocent pleasures, and withal, so sound a judgment, both concerning men and things, had made this northern tour instead of Franck ; and had detailed in the beautiful simplicity of his Arcadian language, his observations on the scenery and manners of Scotland."

Revenge was the last thing Walton would care for ; but what a revenge time brought for him ! Here is the greatest genius of Scotland editing the only other edition of Franck's book ever published, and in the lines I have just quoted wishing Walton had made the journey and written the book.   Still, one cannot help agreeing with Sir Walter that the gibes of Franck at " that scribbling putationer *The Compleat Angler* " are none the less pungent for having some substratum of truth in so far as they are the sarcasms of one who did know and practise fly-fishing for both salmon and trout, whereas Walton does not pretend to have done any salmon-

fishing with the fly-rod—that, as Sir
Walter calls it, "noble branch of the art,
which exceeds all other uses of the
angling-rod, as much as fox-hunting
excels hare-hunting."

Franck insinuates more than once that
Walton's book owes its popularity to its
instructions how to cook fish rather than
how to catch them ; in fact, he says plainly
in one place that Walton's arguments
would " beyond dispute have undubitably
miscarried had not his wife had a finger
in the pie."

J. R. Lowell's " Introduction " to Walton.

The latest " Introduction " to an edition
of Walton is one of the most important,
as it contains the critical opinion of the
man and the book by no less a writer
than James Russell Lowell. I confess
that the pleasure with which I read the
announcement that the author of *The
Biglow Papers* was to write this very
charming essay was not quite realised.
In spite of much which every lover of
Walton must re-echo, there are one or two
things which seem to leave a somewhat
unpleasant flavour in the mouth : this, for
instance, referring to some men Walton

knew, such as Carey, Brome, and Ben
Jonson :—

"But these less reputable intimates he
made welcome in a back-parlour of his
mind, away from the street and with the
curtains drawn, as if he would fain hide
them even from himself."

Again : "Those must have been delightful evenings which the two friends [Walton
and Cotton] spent together after the day's
fishing. Well into the night they must
have lingered with much excellent discourse of books and men, now serious,
now playful—much personal anecdote and
reminiscence. Perhaps it was as well that
Dr. Morley should be at Winchester—with
all respect be it said, and not forgetting
that Walton has told us he 'loved such
mirth as did not make friends ashamed to
look upon one another next morning.'"

Again, I can see nothing to make it an
indication of a "lower love" that Walton
"takes care to tell us that a certain artificial
fly" (minnow it was) "was made by a handsome woman and with a fine hand."

Of Walton's style the critic says :
"Walton, at any rate, in course of time,
attained, at least in prose, to something
which, if it may not be called style, was
a very charming way of writing, all the
more so that he has an innocent air of

not knowing how it is done. . . . No man ever achieved, as Walton sometimes did, a simplicity which leaves criticism helpless by the mere light of nature alone."

In another place, in referring to an account Walton gives of an accidental meeting with Sanderson, Mr. Lowell says, " It is exactly as if he were telling us of it, and this sweet persuasiveness of the living and naturally cadenced voice is never wanting in Walton. It is indeed his distinction, and it is a very rare quality in writers, upon most of whom, if they ever happily forget themselves and fall into the tone of talk, the pen too soon comes sputtering in."

His biographical work Mr. Lowell thinks "very delightful; and though more rambling than Plutarch, comes nearer to him than any other life-writing I can think of. . . . Never, surely, was there a more lovable man, nor to whom love found access by more avenues of sympathy. There are two books which have a place by themselves and side by side in our literature, Walton's *Compleat Angler* and White's *Natural History of Selborne.* . . . The purely literary charm of neither of them will alone authorise the place they hold so securely, though, as respects the *Angler,* this charm must be taken more largely into account.

. . . They have this in common, that those who love them find themselves growing more and more to love the authors of them too. Theirs is an immortality of affection, perhaps the most desirable, as it is the rarest, of all. . . . Both these books are pre-eminently cheerful books, and have the invaluable secret of distilling sunshine out of leaden skies. . . . If I must seek a word that more than any other explains the pleasure which Walton's way of writing gives us, I should say it was its innocency. It refreshes like the society of children."

I ought not to omit mention of the edition of Walton published at threepence in Cassell's " National Library," especially as the editor, Professor Henry Morley, LL.D., says, " There was but one Izaak Walton ; and his book has an undying charm."

And here I must conclude this rambling little excursion among some old angling writers. I have cast my fly among their pages and the pages of those who have written of them ; and if my work has any value, it will be in the variety and interest of the extracts given. It is, as I said when commencing it, written, not for those who know Walton's writings, but in the hope that it may induce some who do not to become acquainted with them. I had intended to have referred at some length to the Lives, but have already exceeded the space at my disposal. One final cast before putting up my pen.

"There are no colours in the fairest sky
  So fair as these; the feather whence the pen
  Was shaped that traced the lives of these
      good Men,
  Dropped from an angel's wing. With moist-
      ened eye,
  We read of faith and purest charity,
  In Statesman, Priest, and humble Citizen.
  Oh! could we copy their mild virtues, then
  What joy to live; what blessedness to die!
  Methinks their very Names shine still and
      bright,
  Apart — like glow-worms in the woods of
      spring,
  Or lonely tapers shooting far a light
  That guides and cheers—or, seen like stars on
      high,
  Satellites burning in a lucid ring,
  Around meek Walton's heavenly memory."

  WORDSWORTH's *Sonnet on Walton's Lives.*

" It might sweeten a man's temper at any time to read *The Compleat Angler.*"—CHARLES LAMB.

FINIS.

INDEX.

Elliot Stock, Paternoster Row, London.

"The noblest gift-book that has been issued for many years."—*St. James's Gazette.*

The LEA and DOVE EDITION, being the 100th
EDITION of

THE COMPLEAT ANGLER.

Edited by R. B. MARSTON,

*Editor of the "Fishing Gazette"; Hon. Treasurer
of the Fly-Fishers' Club.*

The principal feature of this Edition is a Set of 54 Full-page Photogravures, printed from Copper-plates on fine Plate Paper, of Views on the Lea, Dove, Etc., and about 100 other Illustrations, all made for this Edition.

LARGE PAPER EDITION, in 2 Vols. Royal Quarto, bound in full-morocco, each copy numbered and signed, £10 10s.

The DEMY QUARTO EDITION, bound in half-morocco, gilt top, **£5 5s.**

The whole of the type of this Edition has been distributed and the Full-page Copper-plates destroyed.

Very few copies of the Five-Guinea and only one or two of the Ten-Guinea Edition remain for sale.

From a long Review in the *Times*, Sept. 4th, 1889:—
"The edition which celebrates the centenary of 'The Compleat Angler' is altogether worthy of the immortal work. Mr. Marston, the Editor of the *Fishing Gazette*, who is known as a 'deacon of the craft,' has grudged neither time, nor money, nor labour in perfecting these two magnificent volumes. The type and paper make a masterpiece of mechanical work, and the exquisite photogravures with which the volumes are embellished leave little or nothing to be desired."

"Never has Walton been more honoured. . . . It will be one of the forms in which the work of Walton will be most coveted."—*Standard.*

"These sumptuous volumes."—*Spectator.*

"A truly magnificent edition."—*Field.*

Press Notices of the 100th Edition of "The Compleat Angler" (*continued*).

" This noble edition."—*Daily News.*

"So well graced a book will be in great demand among book collectors and anglers. It is the most desirable edition of Walton that has ever been offered to the public."—*Scotsman.*

" There are thousands upon thousands of anglers to whom the possession of such sumptuous volumes would be a lifelong joy ; but for most of them the work is too costly, and the edition is limited ! Let us hope that the copies will fall into such hands only as Izaak Walton would have himself approved. They are 'a dish of meat too good for any but anglers or honest men,' and we can only hope that those who are fortunate enough to place these volumes upon their shelves ' will prove both.' "—*Saturday Review.*

" It is not merely the finest tribute yet paid to the wide and lasting popularity of Izaak Walton's book, but it is in itself a treasure of printing, binding, and illustration. To the reverent and loving care of Mr. R. B. Marston, one of the partners in the publishing house, and a well-known master of the gentle art, this new issue, henceforth to be known as the 'Lea and Dove Edition,' is due. . . . Mr. Marston's introductory notes, while full of valuable information, are most pleasant reading, and the two volumes are a standing credit to all concerned in their production."—*The World.*

"A work by which the English printing industry and publishing enterprise of the later nineteenth century might well consent to be represented before the severest æsthetic tribunal of posterity. For clear-cut beauty of typography, for sober richness of binding and decoration, for lavish wealth and artistic excellence of illustration, it is a veritable triumph of the arts which have co-operated in its production. . . . No more magnificent tribute has ever been paid to the name and fame of an English classic than this."—*Daily Telegraph.*

" This magnificent publication is second in interest to no predecessor in the long list of editions contained in the 'Chronicle of the Compleat Angler.' "—*Pall Mall Gazette.*

"This admirable edition."—*Morning Post.*

LONDON:

SAMPSON LOW, MARSTON, AND COMPANY, LD.,
St. Dunstan's House, Fetter Lane, Fleet Street, E.C.